SWEETHEART WEDDING

A Cranberry Bay Book

MINDY HARDWICK

Story Blurb

Determined to start her life over after a failed engagement, Gracie has built her boutique inn into a successful Cranberry Bay business. Meanwhile, youngest Shuster brother, Adam, loves helping his friends and family while working as a park ranger. Devastated after a tragic accident, Adam guards his heart and is happy to have Gracie's friendship. Both swear off love. But when Adam and Gracie are tossed together to help plan a Cranberry Bay wedding, they find their resolve not to fall in love crumbling. And when Adam loses his Oregon State Parks job and takes a new job in Montana, both will have to decide whether to make the commitment to love each other and leave Cranberry Bay behind for a new life.

PRINT ISBN: 979-8-218-67530-1

August 2025

Developmental Editor: Bev Katz Rosenbaum
Copy Editor: Heart Full of Ink, Casey Harris-Parks
Cover Artist: Su Kopil, Earthly Charms
Book Format and Layout: Eagle Bay Press

Eagle Bay Press
P.O. Box 1391
Cannon Beach, Oregon. 97110

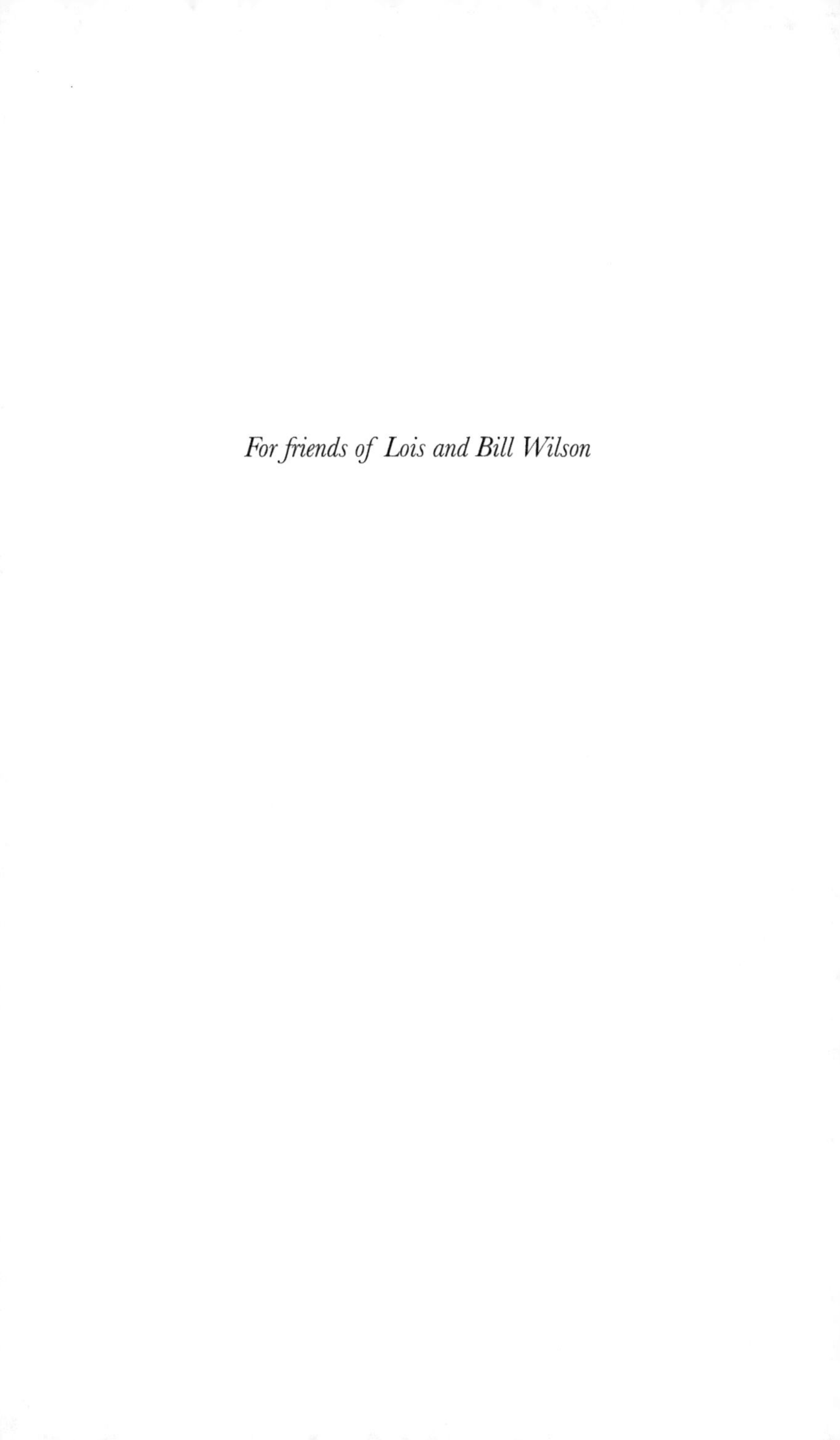

For friends of Lois and Bill Wilson

Cast of Characters

<u>Shuster Family</u>

Rebecca: Mother. Husband died of a heart attack. Retired librarian.

Sawyer: Oldest brother. Land Developer. Married to Katie

Lauren: Sawyer's daughter. Ten-years-old. Mother died of cancer.

Bryan Shuster. Middle Brother. Real Estate agent. Married to Rylee.

Adam Shuster: Youngest Brother. Park Ranger. Friends with Josh Morton

Lisa Shuster: Single mother to daughter Maddie. Lives in carriage house on Sawyer's property.

Maddie: Sixteen-year-old daughter of Lisa.

<u>Sewing Circle</u>

Katie Coos: Owns the Fabric and Sewing Barn. Married to Sawyer

Rylee Harper: Owns the River Cottages. Married to Bryan, her childhood sweetheart. Owns dog, Raisin.

Ivy Moore: Owns the Red Door Antique Shop. Married to Josh Morton.

Gracie Catskill: Owns the New Leaf Inn. Excellent embroidery.

Sasha Frazier: Owns the Lazy Dayz Bakery. Single Mother to ten-year-old Tyler. Married to Greg Matthews.

Tyler: Ten-year old son to Sasha. Dad is Greg Matthews who he doesn't know.

Chapter 1

Adam tapped his fingers on the steering wheel. The line of cars in front of him on Highway 101 didn't move. He fiddled with his cell phone, pulling up the traffic cam app. It showed three cars pulled over to the side at mile marker 10. He'd been driving Highway 101 since he was sixteen, going from Cranberry Bay to the Seashore Cove Aquarium, where he got his first job. During the summer the highway became a parking lot of cars trying to get to the beach towns. But it was mid-May, still the shoulder season. He'd just passed mile marker 20. Ten miles to go to Cranberry Bay.

His phone buzzed. Angie, the Wildlife Center's office manager's name, flashed across his screen. He flicked the button on his steering wheel allowing the call through Bluetooth. Angie's husband, Bill, volunteered as the Wildlife Center's veterinarian. The Wildlife Center ran on a tight budget based on donations and grants, and everyone except Angie worked as a volunteer.

"There's an injured seabird," Angie said, her voice breathless.

"Is Gracie available to pick up the bird?" Adam took a deep breath. There were a handful of volunteers up and down the North Oregon Coast who responded to the seabird rescue requests. Most of the folks were retired and had the time to learn how to rescue an injured seabird, respond to the call and then drive the seabird in a box or small crate to the Wildlife Center. Even though she wasn't one of the retired volunteers, Gracie was Adam's top choice for bird transport volunteers. They'd become friends after Gracie moved to Cranberry Bay and joined the Cranberry Bay sewing circle. The women convinced Gracie she needed a hiking partner and introduced her to Adam, a park ranger and brother-in-law to Katie and Rylee. People often asked if they were dating, but both had declared it was only a friendship and there was nothing romantic between them.

"I couldn't reach anyone," Angie said. "It's the Literature Festival in Sea Shore Cove. Everyone is listening to authors and not responding to their cell phones. Where are you?"

Adam gripped the steering wheel. "Stuck in traffic. There's a stalled vehicle or accident about ten miles up. Where is the bird?" He ran through the slogans from his AA meetings. *First Things First. Easy Does It.* He'd been sober for five years and most of the time he didn't have a craving to drink. But high-tension moments where failure was possible could still cause the craving to return.

"Seashore Cove," Angie said. "I was hoping you could get to it."

"It's going to be a while if the traffic doesn't start moving," Adam said. "What type of bird?"

"Tufted puffin."

Adam tightened his jaw. The tufted puffin was a species of concern. Their numbers dwindled each year as many didn't return to nest on the large sea stack jutting out of the ocean. The large rock had been their nesting ground for decades. Each spring, the tufted puffins returned to their burrows and laid a single egg. The puffins stayed on the rock until early August when they would return to sea. There had been a few puffin studies done over the years, and the general conclusion was they couldn't find a food source at sea and were starving.

The traffic ahead of Adam inched forward. "We're moving. Slowly. But the traffic is moving."

"I hope you make it," Angie said. "The Wildlife Center could use the positive publicity." A loud bird call sounded behind Angie. "Gotta go. We've got a rescue coming in."

Adam knew all too well about the negative press the Wildlife Center had received over the last month. The Wildlife Center's social media had been filled with comments about how the Center had missed taking in an injured bird. They didn't have the volunteers to keep the center open over the weekend and injured birds could often end up not making it. He'd been acting as the center's volunteer director while the board worked to raise funds to hire someone. He'd done his best to respond to every comment on social media, but it hadn't stopped the negativity from taking over their pages. The fundraising had gone slowly over the last year and a half, and he'd juggled his full-time job as a state park ranger with his Wildlife Center responsibilities. If it wasn't for Angie, the Wildlife Center would have closed. But she'd thrown her weight behind the Wildlife Center and spent countless unpaid hours working to make sure someone was on hand to receive the injured birds as well as facilitate care for the birds with her husband, Bill, a volunteer veterinarian who specialized in sea birds.

He tapped his fingers on the steering wheel as the cars inched forward. The AA slogan played in his head. *Easy Does It.* In the past, he would have pulled off and popped into the nearest tavern. One drink would become six or seven and before he knew it the pub would be closing, and someone would put him into a ride share. He'd wake up the next morning, not knowing what happened and trying to pretend he did. But AA taught him he had a daily reprieve from drinking if he remembered to turn the day over to his Higher Power, call his sponsor, and attend meetings, he could keep that sobriety one more day.

Ahead, a series of lights flashed. It looked like an accident and not a stalled vehicle.

Adam loved the Wildlife Center but they had a series of unfortunate timing. The center lost a large Brown Pelican, a Cormorant, and a couple Western Gulls. The birds had all been dropped off by well-meaning citizens who had come upon them while walking the beach. Usually, when the birds were dropped off, there was someone to intake them. But Angie and Bill had been at her sister's wedding in Portland for a few days and there was no one to take them in. By the time the birds were admitted, they were too far gone to be rescued, despite Bill's best efforts.

The news media had gotten hold of the story and released a series of sensationalized stories which had been shared all over social media in minutes. The public outcry had been one of disbelief and outrage. Adam, Angie, Bill, and the few people on the Board of Directors had been dismayed by the lack of community under-standing of the dire situation.

The center couldn't afford to lose another seabird, especially a tufted puffin. Sea Shore Cove had the puffin as their mascot bird. T-shirts, logos, and a small emblem on the entrance to Seashore Cove, along with an annual Welcome Back Puffin festival.

Traffic moved forward and Adam's chest tightened. The memories lodged in his throat. Another rescue he didn't get to in time. A rescue where he'd lost not a seabird but a person. A kayak accident in Cranberry Bay that haunted him, pushing him to drink away his pain until even that hadn't worked. Then his brothers had gathered around him and, with an intervention, forced him to see what he was doing. He chose to go to rehab and attend AA.

"Easy does it." He exhaled and spoke the slogan he

knew so well from the rooms of AA into the confines of the car.

Mile marker nine. Eight. Seven. He was making progress.

And then brake lights. Adam hit the steering wheel hard. He picked up his cell phone and punched in Gracie's name. He hoped she could rescue the injured bird.

The phone barely rang. "Hello. Adam?" Gracie's soft, smooth voice filled his ear. Just hearing her calm tone settled his racing heart and anxious stomach.

"There's an injured bird," Adam said. "None of the volunteers can get there and I'm stuck in traffic."

"Where?"

"Seashore Cove. It's on the south end of the beach. An eagle must have picked it off the sea rock and dropped it. The caller told Angie the bird was stunned but alive."

"Give me five minutes," Gracie said. "I've got an empty box and a towel ready."

"It's a tufted puffin," Adam said. Traffic moved in front of him.

Gracie inhaled. "I'm on my way."

"I'll meet you as soon as I can." Adam swallowed. "Thanks, Gracie."

"Of course."

He tapped the button to end the call and exhaled. Gracie would get there. She wasn't an official volunteer for the Wildlife Center. She couldn't commit to the regular calls along with running her New Leaf Inn. But she walked the beach every day and Adam had trained her on how to rescue a bird. She kept the supplies in her car, a blanket, a towel, a small box, and a cat carrier. The bigger pelicans always needed a larger container, but most of the volunteers didn't carry them because those rescues weren't that common. Most of the birds, the seagulls, the cormorants, the common murres, and occasionally, a tufted puffin, only needed a small box or cat carrier.

Traffic moved and Adam worked his way past the three-car fender bender accident. A woman stood outside her car, waving her arms. A man talked into a cell phone alongside his car. Adam didn't recognize either, but that wasn't uncommon. Highway 101 spanned from Pelican Shores all the way down the Oregon Coast. People from Pelican Shores, Sea Shore Cove, and Cranberry Bay all traveled on it frequently.

He nodded to Officer Perkins from Sea Shore Cove, who talked to a heavy-set man standing beside a minivan and a tow truck. Officer Pekins had given him a ride home from the Sea Shore Cove pub on more than a few occasions. He never blamed or shamed Adam. One morning, he'd shown up at Adam's trailer with a coffee and some AA literature. He'd talked to Adam about AA and how it could help him. But Adam hadn't been ready to hear it.

A few months later, when he'd gone to his first AA meeting after the intervention, Officer Perkins greeted him with a hug and a cup of coffee and invited him to sit beside him at the meeting.

Adam pressed hard on the ignition and in seven minutes pulled into the parking lot of the south beach access in Seashore Cove. He slipped his Wildlife Center badge onto the rearview mirror and made sure the bright yellow card with the white lettering faced outward. Emergency vehicles were the only cars allowed on the North Oregon Coast beach.

There were a couple ramps for emergency personnel to reach all parts of the three-mile beach. Most of the time, the accidents were minor. A sprained ankle. A hurt dog. In the summer months, emergency sirens could usually be heard once a day for a stranded hiker on the rocky cliffs above the ocean or the occasional surfer who got in trouble in the cold waters.

But Adam didn't rescue people. He stopped giving kayak tours after the accident. He didn't trust himself to ever have someone in his care who he might need to rescue. He stuck to birds.

Adam drove slowly down the beach, looking for Gracie with the tufted puffin. This was always the hardest part of rescue and transport—finding the volunteer and the bird on the wide expansive beach. Thankfully, the mid-week spring day hadn't brought out the summer crowds.

A woman wearing a green knit cap sat on a driftwood log. Something wrapped in a bright orange towel held between her legs. Adam angled his truck toward them. In seconds, he pulled up alongside Gracie. Adam grabbed the small animal carrier from the passenger seat. He pulled on a thick pair of work gloves, opened the door and stepped out.

Gracie's white Westie, Max, sat beside her, the dog's eyes alert as he scanned the horizon. Gracie had trained the dog well and he knew not to bother the injured bird. It always disturbed Adam when saw dogs chasing seagulls down the beach. Dogs could be off-leash on the spacious Oregon Coast beaches, but they had to be under voice control, something the tourists and occasionally local people forgot.

"Thanks for helping, Gracie." His spirits lifted as he smiled at Gracie. Her friendship was one of the biggest things he was grateful for. She always made him feel happy. Adam opened the cat carrier and set it on the sand. Cat carriers were the perfect size for most of the shore birds, with the exception of the Brown Pelicans, who had to be carted off the beach in large boxes or open plastic tubs, due to their wingspan. Thankfully, they didn't get that many pelican bird rescues.

Adam lifted the wrapped bird from Gracie's lap. The bird shifted against his hands but didn't struggle. He placed it gently inside the crate.

"What are the chances of survival?" Gracie's sharp and inquisitive blue eyes searched his. Gracie questioned almost everything, but he enjoyed the way she didn't just take information at face value. She mulled it over and considered every side.

"It depends." Adam snapped the enclosure shut. "If the bird hasn't been on the beach for too long then we have a good shot."

"Eagle." Gracie pointed to a tall set of trees behind them. "It probably is the same one who plucked this puffin off the sea rock."

"Good eye." Adam followed Gracie's hand and looked upward.

All spring, the eagles had been determined to snatch any bird they could off the large sea stack. At times, two of them perched on top of the sea stack forcing the other birds off the rock in large groups, squawking and calling. Nature and its rules. Adam learned long ago to respect them.

"Time to go, Max." Gracie lifted Max's leather leash from one of the logs. The beach was covered with logs that rolled in during the winter storms. As the summer season started, the logs would become bonfires along the wide-open Oregon Coast. And as it heated up in August, those same bonfires would be set up too close to the dry driftwood lining the dunes. Adam would spend the evenings working as an extra park ranger, patrolling the shore to make sure the bonfires weren't lit and didn't start a wildfire with a spark flying into the tall grasses.

Gracie and Max walked beside Adam as he carried the crate to the passenger side of his truck. He opened the door and placed the carrier on the seat. Shutting the door, he turned to Gracie and slipped his hands into his pockets. Sometimes he felt like he was eighteen again when he was around Gracie.

"I'm sure Mom and everyone would love to see you on Sunday for brunch." He bit back the words that *he* would love to see her on Sunday for brunch. He was never quite sure how far to push their friendship and the last thing he ever wanted was to lose it.

"I would love to see her and the Shuster family, too. Should I bring my cheese grits?" Gracie asked and smiled at him. Gracie's cheese grits were legendary in Cranberry Bay.

"We love your cheese grits. Everyone should be there this week." Adam was the youngest Shuster brother. Over the last few years, he'd watched as both his brothers had found the loves of their lives. Sawyer fell in love with his business competitor Katie. Even though Katie's sewing shop had closed, she reestablished herself in a renovated old barn on Sawyer's property, offering sewing classes and weekend retreats, which were popular with sewers and quilters across the United States.

His middle brother, Bryan, had married his high school sweetheart, Rylee, when she moved back to Cranberry Bay to take care of her grandmother's home. Rylee had renovated the old fishing cottages on the bay into charming vintage cottage rentals. They were fully booked for the next few months.

And Josh, the beloved not-a-blood-brother but long-time friend of the Shuster brothers married Ivy, owner of the Cranberry Bay Antique shop and they had a one-year-old daughter.

Rounding off the weekly Sunday brunch were his mom, Rebeca Shuster, and longtime family friend and lawyer, Jack Sutton. As the only single Shuster brother, and after his friendship with Gracie had developed, they encouraged him to invite Gracie to their family brunches.

Adam's phone beeped and the number for the Wildlife Center flashed across the screen.

"Hey Angie," Adam said. "I've got the puffin and will be heading your way."

Angie's clear voice spoke into his ear, giving him instructions about which cage would be ready. When she finished, Adam clicked off his phone and slipped it into his pocket.

"Will there be ten people including us at the brunch?" Gracie counted on her fingers. "Yes," Adam said. Ten people."

Something in her voice made Adam pause. Gracie had been in Cranberry Bay for two years and she built a successful boutique inn out of the run-down motel that used to be on Main Street. But sometimes, he heard pain in her voice. A pain she never talked about. Sometimes, Gracie reminded him of the handful of birds that were never released back into the wild due to an injury that made it impossible for them to survive on their own.

One of the Wildlife Center's favorite sea birds, a Cormorant, had been picked up by an eagle and dropped as a young bird a few years ago. The Cormorant had been rescued and taken to the Wildlife Center where it recovered and learned to trust its humans.

But Adam also had his own pain, a pain that never quite went away. A pain from failing to rescue a teen on the bay in a kayak. That pain had caused him to live with guilt that was overwhelming. He'd started drinking heavily and his longtime girlfriend left him, something he didn't fault her for. He could barely live in his own skin during the drinking, but he couldn't stop. He needed something to numb the pain of the failed rescue and once he started drinking more drinks followed until he felt numb. Eventually, Sawyer and Bryan staged an intervention and took him to treatment and regular AA meetings. He'd been able to come to terms with his past and chart a course forward in his life. But the failed rescue convinced him that he could never fall in love again and not be able to save someone he loved. It was why his friendship with Gracie worked so well.

"See you at brunch." Gracie touched Adam on the arm. He lifted his hand and touched the top of hers. Their eyes met and that feeling of being eighteen and having a crush flooded him. Then, just as quickly, both dropped their hands and looked away.

Chapter 2

Gracie shook a pebble out of her hiking boot and dropped the boot on the inn's porch. Stepping inside, she unhooked Max's leash and hung it on one of the pegs by the front entryway closet. Max trotted down the hall toward the kitchen and his water bowl. She slipped into her soft soled slippers and padded across the hardwood floor of the front entryway.

The phone had been ringing for the last minute, and she headed toward the front desk to answer it. At the same time, the bell over the front door chimed and two couples walked in. They greeted her and walked up the stairs to their second-floor room.

Gracie ran her hands through her hair. She really needed to hire someone to help her part-time. Ever since Rylee and Bryan's Riverside Cottages had been profiled in the state's travel magazine, the small town of Cranberry Bay found itself overflowing with visitors and not enough places to stay. But finding people to work was difficult. Affordable housing was in short supply and there was a worker shortage up and down the coast. She was lucky Maddie, Sawyer and Katie's seventeen-year-old niece, helped clean the rooms on busy weekends.

"Hello!"

Gracie whirled around, the words on the tip of her tongue to say the inn had no vacancy for tonight. The two-story building included eight bedrooms, two with shared baths, a small suite with a kitchenette that she often rented to one of the students working at the environmental beach program in Seashore Cove, and her own suite tucked in the far corner of the building. She hoped to renovate the backyard into a courtyard where she could serve afternoon tea and host a few private events, but she needed more time and workers to accomplish those goals.

"Aunt Celia!" Gracie said. Her aunt's blue eyes sparkled as she peered at her over her rhinestone glasses. She wore one of her trademark colorful scarves draped around her neck, and a flowy green blouse draped over dark jeans. Her red painted toenails peeked out from green sandals.

"Do you have room for your old Aunt?" She held out her arms and Gracie stepped into the circle of her aunt's warmth.

"Of course!" Gracie hid the quick flick of panic racing through her stomach as she stepped away from her aunt and looked at the large reservation book. Gracie refused to use the computer to make reservations for her clients after her last computer crashed during a winter windstorm. Ivy found the leather book in her stash of antique shop donations, and she'd given it to Gracie. "I thought you were coming next week. I don't have any open rooms."

"My plans changed a bit." Aunt Celia shrugged out of her long purple cape. "You have room in your home, yes?"

Gracie frowned. She had converted a couple of rooms on the second floor into a small apartment for herself. The rooms were cozy and consisted of a bedroom, a small kitchen, and a living room with a bathroom tucked off the living room. Aunt Celia could have the bedroom, and she'd sleep on the couch. She'd never let her aunt down, not after she had supported Gracie through the disaster of her engagement.

"I don't need much room, dear," Aunt Celia said. "But I do need a cup of tea. We are having spring in St. Louis, but I see you are still in winter!"

"Of course. I can light the gas fireplace in the living room if that would help." Spring on the west coast was always chilly. Although the sun came out much more than in the dark winter days, spring warmth didn't arrive until late May, and it was still mid-April.

"No, dear." Aunt Celia waved her away the offer. "Just a cup of tea and then I will sit in that big cozy chair." She pointed to the oversized cream chair next to Gracie's piano.

Gracie busied herself with getting her aunt's tea from a

tray she kept for her guests in the front lobby. Why had she suddenly shown up a week early? And without warning her? Gracie talked to her mom and sister once a week. She'd just talked to them last Sunday. No one had mentioned anything about Aunt Celia. But that wasn't unusual. Aunt Celia kept to herself, and it was only Gracie who had become close with her aunt when Aunt Celia supported her.

The front door burst open. Sasha and Katie stepped inside the entryway, their arms filled with thick wedding books. Rylee trailed behind with a stack of library books in her arms. Rebecca Shuster, the town's librarian and mother to the three Shuster brothers, had obviously allowed more than the allotted book five-book check out rule. Katie, Rylee, and Sasha were all part of the women's sewing circle that met at least once a week to work on sewing projects, discuss upcoming Cranberry Bay events, and enjoy each other's friendship. Gracie looked forward to their get togethers each week.

Gracie smiled at her friends but her stomach churned. It'd been nothing but wedding talk for the last month. Over the last two years, she watched as each of her friends had gotten married. Rylee to the middle Shuster brother, Bryan, Katie to the oldest Shuster brother, Sawyer, and Ivy to the long-time best friend of the Shuster brothers, Josh.

Now, it was Sasha and Greg's turn. Sasha owned the town bakery and had been part of the women's sewing circle for a long time. Gracie was happy for Sasha and Greg. They'd been apart for ten years and recently reunited, falling in love all over again. They were both determined to give their son, Tyler, a home.

Sasha wanted a themed vintage wedding, 1950s style and all of them were having a great time planning ideas, laughing over the full circle skirt dresses in tulle and satin, recommending favorite rock'n'roll tunes for the reception, and questioning if they needed to wear the little white gloves during the entire wedding reception or if the ceremony would be enough.

But something inside Gracie felt like the stomach flu. Something she tried to push down but it never quite left her. The wedding. The wedding she never had to the man who she believed she loved. Except for the cruel words and abuse he so strategically placed on spots she could easily cover with sleeves and pants. It was always after drinking.

When she met him, she thought he just liked to party. As their relationship progressed and she watched the black mood descend and deepen as he polished off bottles of scotch, it became obvious that he struggled with a drinking problem. She had tried everything to make him stop. She'd poured alcohol down the sink, pleaded, begged, and withheld her love. None of it worked for very long and she felt unable to leave him, afraid of what might happen if she did.

Ashamed of herself and her inability to leave him, she'd gotten caught in the cycle of abuse, unable to leave the entrapment of his promises that he would stop the drinking and the hitting, along with the elaborate gifts he'd buy her. Until he left her two days before her wedding, telling her he was in love with someone else.

Determined not to fall apart, she'd flown to the Oregon Coast for their honeymoon and taken the trip solo. But she only made it as far as Cranberry Bay, stopping at the run-down inn with the for-sale sign. It seemed like the perfect place to mend her broken heart and build a new life in a small town, across the country from St. Louis where she'd grown up. Far away from the memories that plagued her of a betrayed love and the lies she'd told to everyone but especially herself, to keep the abuse and drinking a secret. A shameful secret.

Gracie jerked herself out of her thoughts as the phone rang again. Grateful for the distraction, she hurried to the front desk. "New Leaf Inn, this is Gracie."

Gracie listened as the woman on the other end chatted about a mother-daughter reservation for August. Gracie flipped through the reservation book and made a note for the mother and daughter to share the Sunflower and Daisy rooms on the second floor during the second week of August.

After she confirmed the reservation, she set down the phone and turned back to the living room. Sasha and Katie had spread the wedding dress books across the large coffee table and pored over the glossy pictures. Katie took notes for the poofy veil and full skirted wedding dress she would sew for Sasha. As one of the best clothing designers on the coast, she'd offered to sew not only the wedding dress but also the bridesmaids' dresses. Aunt

Celia sipped a cup of tea and chatted with the girls about her mother's wedding—a wedding held in the 1950s in a large ballroom in a St. Louis downtown hotel.

Gracie wandered over and stood behind Aunt Celia. She plastered one of her famous smiles on her face and tried to push away the feeling inside her. The last thing she wanted to do was ruin the wedding of one of her closest friends. She'd made it through her other friends' weddings and hadn't felt this amount of emotion. But she hadn't played as big a part of those weddings. Sasha was one of her closest friends. The two had bonded over the trials and tribulations of trying to run a business in the small town of Cranberry Bay. Sasha's bakery seemed to run effortlessly, but Gracie knew the long hours Sasha worked wearing multiple hats for the business. They often shared their worries, fears, and joys about their businesses over late-night day-old pastries and tea.

Outside, a motorcycle cruising down Main Street revved its engine and the feeling inside Gracie's stomach intensified. Mike, her ex-fiancé, had driven a motorcycle. The noise reminded her of their fights when they were dating when he would leave her, leaning against the wall, clutching her stomach or her face, or wherever his fists had landed. He had stormed out to his motorcycle and roared off, most of the time after he'd been drinking. She would lie awake, worrying about his safety as he drove to his favorite bar. The next day, he'd return, flowers in hand, another apology and the promise that it would never happen again. Empty promises. But she had believed them, not wanting to see the truth about the man she loved.

"Gracie."

With a start, she realized Rylee had been calling her name.

"I'm sorry." Gracie shook her head.

"Is everything okay?" Rylee peered at her.

"Of course." Gracie smiled, hoping the smile would convince Rylee she'd just been distracted. "I just have too much on my mind." She wanted to trust her friends and tell them everything. The women in the sewing circle had never done anything to prove they were not trustworthy. They knew she'd been betrayed at the altar, but she never talked about the abuse or drinking. She'd kept that hidden, tucked inside far away from everyone. It seemed so shameful, something she should have known better and left sooner.

She was an educated woman. She attended yearly fundraisers for women's causes and helped raise money for shelters. And yet she'd stayed in her own abusive relationship, telling no one and reaffirming to herself that she loved him and it would all stop one day.

When she first arrived in Cranberry Bay, unlike the nearby popular coastal towns, Cranberry Bay seemed like a ghost town. The run-down buildings and homes mirrored the way she felt inside. When she'd pulled in front of a large two-story brick building with a For Sale sign in front of it, Gracie made a phone call and within hours she had a bid on the run-down former Cranberry Bay Hotel. Her job as a real estate agent had given her a healthy savings account, a savings account she believed she was saving for children one day. But those dreams were gone and by the end of the week, with inspections finished and bank paperwork complete, she was the new owner of the small hotel with enough of a bank account remaining to decorate the rooms and paint the lower living areas.

She had her beloved piano shipped from St. Louis and enjoyed spending evenings playing songs she'd loved in the brightly lit yellow living room.

She joined the church choir and played music for Sunday services, fulfilling her love of music. And when she could, she slipped away to walk the trails. The sewing circle had been worried about her solo hikes and introduced her to the youngest Shuster brother, Adam, who worked as a park ranger when he wasn't volunteering at the local wildlife center. The two had struck up a friendship, both finding their love of hiking a bonding point. And neither expressed an interest in having anything more than a friendship.

The inn never made a lot of money, but it made enough for her to keep it going. And in the two years she'd been in Cranberry Bay, she'd rebuilt her life in the small town, a town where everyone looked out for each other, and it felt like family. She couldn't imagine living anywhere else.

Rylee frowned as her phone beeped again. "Apparently, there's a large event going on in Seashore Cove the same weekend as your wedding, Sasha."

"It's the Savor Seashore Cove event. In the last couple

years, it's sold out every hotel in town," Katie said. "People like their local Oregon wines!"

"We've even been getting calls for reservations," Gracie said. "Of course," she smiled at Sasha, "the hotel's rooms have been reserved for the wedding guests. Greg's mom and cousins." She ticked the names off on her list.

"It was our only date." Sasha raised her hands in mock surrender, her gold engagement ring flashing in the light. "Greg booked our honeymoon to Europe before we checked the calendar for the big events in Seashore Cove." She shook her head. "I'm still teaching him how things work in small towns. He's so used to his assistant scheduling everything for him in Seattle where there are plenty of options."

Gracie smiled. She knew how hard it had been for Sasha to accept Greg's love. They'd known each other in college when Sasha got pregnant. At the same time, she'd lost her scholarship and had to leave college. By the time she realized she was pregnant, she decided not to tell Greg for fear of interrupting his path to success with an unwanted baby. But after ten years, with a successful career as an investor, Greg had shown up in Cranberry Bay, wanting to buy the marina and found Sasha and Tyler. Gradually, he'd won Sasha's love and she surrendered to him and his support, including the ability to take her wherever she wanted to go on her honeymoon.

"Don't forget I'm baking the cake," Sasha said.

"We're looking forward to your cake," Gracie said. Sasha loved her bakery. She'd allowed Greg to purchase a

couple major appliances she needed and a new refur-
bished vintage trailer for events. She insisted she'd still
run the bakery. But now, Tyler could spend mornings
sleeping and enjoy breakfast and getting off to school
with Greg and not sitting at the bakery at 5 AM while she
baked the pastries for the day.

"What kind of cake are you baking?" Rylee said and
frowned. "Are you sure you want to bake your own
wedding cake?"

"Yes," Sasha said, her voice firm and strong. "I'm
going to bake a ring cake."

"A what?" Rylee asked. Rylee's wedding to Bryan had
been simple, yet traditional. The former high school
sweethearts had reunited when Rylee moved to Cranberry Bay to sell her grandmother's home.

"A ring cake," Sasha said, grinning. "It's two circles
that are linked and our names will be on either side of it."

"I've heard of this kind of cake," Katie said. "There
will be fortunes inside, right?" Katie's own wedding had
been the talk of the town. She married Sawyer, the best
businessman on the coast. The two of them had created
a paradise on his sprawling property north of town. The
entire town had been invited to celebrate not only the
wedding of two of the town's best businesspeople, but
also the joining of their businesses. Katie's sewing shop
expanded into workshops and retreats thanks to the new
buildings Sawyer had built on his property.

"Fortunes?" Rylee scrunched her nose. "Why do we
want fortunes at a wedding?" Rylee's scrutiny could
sometimes exasperate all the sewing circle women, but

they loved each other like sisters and chose to overlook each other's quirks.

"Fortunes are fun." Sasha rubbed her hands together and her eyes glowed. "Small items like a ring or a small toy car. We'll tell everyone about it so they don't bite into the cake and find something they shouldn't!" Sasha's eyes glowed.

The front door opened and Bryan ambled in carrying a large white bakery bag. He wore khaki pants, a green pullover shirt, and his trademark Birkenstock sandals. He pulled out one of Sasha's famous large chocolate chip cookies. Rylee smiled at him and took the cookie. He stepped beside her and massaged her shoulders. She relaxed and the tension dripped from her face as she leaned back into him. Bryan settled Rylee in a way that none of them could.

"Gracie?" Adam stepped through the front door. He slipped off his boots and set them beside Gracie's at the front door. He stepped across the rug in his socked feet and stopped beside her.

She smiled at him. Her heart always beat a little faster when she saw Adam, but she pushed it away as only excitement to see her friend. At first, she'd balked at the concern from the women in the sewing circle that she shouldn't hike alone. But when they'd introduced her to Adam, her worries disappeared. That summer, Adam had been working on one of the trails and over the long summer days, she'd gotten to know him. She enjoyed his quiet presence and gradually she found herself laughing again. They never talked about anything personal, and she'd been happy to leave it that way. He harbored his own secrets, secrets that darkened his face and deepened his voice if topics veered too close and she respected that space, knowing it would also keep her secrets tucked away inside her.

"Are you going to share that cookie?" Katie placed her hands on her hips and stared at Rylee.

Rylee laughed and took another bite. "No."

"I'll get cookies for all of us," Gracie said. "It's the time of the day when I set them out for the guests anyway."

She stood and walked to the kitchen, a large room off the living area. Adam followed behind her. She still flinched, just a bit, when someone stepped behind her, never sure if someone would hit her from behind. She always hoped Adam couldn't see the flinches and busied herself at the sink. A large window overlooked the overgrown garden which hid a big gazebo. She hoped to redo the garden and turn it into a space for gatherings and maybe even small weddings. But she simply hadn't had enough time. It seemed that her time was always fragmented into other places—helping out with town music events like the annual Christmas caroling group or filling in for the high school music teacher when she got sick or needed to attend music conferences and events in Portland. And then there was the matter of trying to run the inn without enough help.

Adam pulled out a large flower painted tray from under the counter. She'd bought it from an artist at one of the summer art fairs. She pulled out a matching tin of chocolate chip cookies. She always made sure to have Sasha's chocolate chip cookies on hand for the guests teatime snack.

"I got that," he said as he took the tin out of her hands. His fingers brushed against hers and a small flutter rose through her stomach. She quickly pushed it away. He unscrewed the lid and placed cookies on the tray. Gracie tried not to watch his hands and imagine those same hands running along her body. She shook herself. It was all the talk about the wedding and love. She and Adam were friends. Period. Unaware of the emotional conflict inside her, Adam worked methodically and formed the cookies into a circle,

"Thank you for your help." Gracie pushed a strand of hair out of her eyes. One thing she loved about her friendship with Adam was the courtesy they showed each other, always remembering to say thank you to each other.

Adam reached into the small basket on the edge of the counter and grabbed a scrunchy. He handed it to Gracie and smiled.

"Thank you." Gracie took the scrunchy and pulled up her hair. She never remembered to tie her hair back and had gotten in trouble with the health department for not wearing it tied back. That day had been an extremely frustrating one and it was only hiking up the river trail that she had settled down after the inspector's visit and long list of things she needed to do to pass inspection with the city. Sasha had also struggled with the inspector's reports on her bakery and both of them had spent many hours going over the long lists each were given for their business.

That day, she'd run into Adam while hiking and he'd made her laugh. He'd shown up the next day with a small basket of scrunchies. He'd placed it on the kitchen counter. "Just in case you get any more surprise visits," he said.

Outside the kitchen door, Max barked. Adam walked to the cabinet and grabbed the dry dog food container. He scooped a handful of kibbles into a bowl with dog prints along the side. She opened the door and her white Westie, Max, trotted inside. He whined at Adam and wagged his tail. Gracie's heart warmed. It made her feel good that her dog liked Adam. She'd gotten Max when she moved to Cranberry Bay. He'd been left at the shelter at nine months old as the family moved into housing that didn't allow dogs. She'd immediately fallen in love with him, and he became her constant companion.

Aunt Celia pushed open the kitchen door. "I'm sorry dear," she said. "I don't mean to interrupt. But I think I should make a phone call and go lie down for a little bit. The time zone difference is catching up with me." She paused and looked at Adam.

"Of course," Gracie said, the worry flooding her again about her aunt. She never remembered Aunt Celia needing to lie down. She rose at dawn and spent her day moving between social engagements, volunteer work, and attending evening concerts and art openings.

"I'm Adam." Adam stepped forward and placed his

outstretched hand in front of her. "Can I help you carry something upstairs?"

"That would be wonderful." Aunt Celia winked at Gracie.

Gracie's worries about her aunt were replaced with embarrassment over her assumption that she and Adam were romantically involved. Heat rose through her neck to her face. She'd have to set her aunt straight that Adam was just a friend and that was all she wanted, even if sometimes her body fluttered at his touch. She'd suffered too much pain in love to want to risk it again.

Chapter 3

Adam pulled into the circular driveway of the library. The lights glowed from the large windows in the brick two-story building. The town's library had been a part of his life ever since he was a child and attended story hour. He'd struggled with reading and his mom, the town's long-time librarian, took him to the Saturday morning sessions of Read with a Dog. A black cocker spaniel and his human sat beside Adam and listened as he fumbled through the words of the storybooks. Every Saturday, the same dog and handler patiently listened as he learned to conquer his fear of reading aloud.

He hoped out of his truck, ducked his head against the pouring rain, and headed into the warm building. It wasn't hard to find his mom, Rebecca Shuster. She was surrounded by children on a small mat in the children's section of the library. At sixty-five, Rebecca kept her hair cut short in a pixie bob and insisted on keeping up with coloring it blonde with red highlights. She also loved to frequent the local boutique shops in Seashore Cove.

Adam and his brothers made sure to always tuck gift cards into her stockings at Christmas. Tonight, she wore a pair of black slacks, a white blouse, and a green and yellow scarf tied around her neck. A long gold chain with a drop heart hung from her neck along with matching earrings. Adam waited for her to finish as he browsed the mystery section of the library. He loved reading C.J. Box during his off time and usually walked out of the library with a stack of books. Rebecca would give him many new mysteries she kept tucked away for him so he could read them and write up reviews for the library that Rebecca posted alongside the new books when they went on display.

As the last child darted off the mat and toward the counter to check out books, Rebecca walked over to him and wrapped him in a warm embrace. "Let me get my things," she said and smiled at him. "I'll be just a minute. It's Darcy's turn to close up tonight." She nodded at the tall thin woman checking out books. Cranberry Bay had recently approved a budget increase for the library and Darcy was hired as part time help to shelve and check out books.

Adam nodded and looked around the small room. It hadn't changed much from the days when he was a small child and came for story hour. He loved the books about the woods and creatures. From the large rug in the center of the room, to the rain running off the large glass pane windows, everything had stayed pretty much the same. Including reading with the dogs on Saturday mornings, just like so much of the town of Cranberry Bay.

Although his older brother Sawyer had brought large scale development to some of the surrounding area, their small town had been kept safe from that development thanks to the hard work of Katie Coos and her team of The Friends of Cranberry Bay. Even after her marriage to Sawyer, Katie had pledged to continue to keep big scale development out of the downtown core of Cranberry Bay and was often found at Planning Commission meetings arguing against a petition to bring a big commercial business into town. It was a fight going on up and down the coast, keeping big city development out of the small towns.

Adam unlocked the truck door, and Rebecca opened the passenger door. She picked up the large envelope on the seat and frowned. "What is in Montana?"

Adam swallowed. He knew his mom didn't want him to leave. But he had no choice but to look for jobs outside of Cranberry Bay, not after the State Park layoffs which came without notice a few days ago. The Wildlife Center couldn't pay a full-time salary for a new director, and he needed health care benefits.

"A great opportunity," Adam said. "Great Falls is looking for someone to help develop a newly acquired property into an educational center with conservation and wildlife rescue." With all the recent layoffs in the federal and state parks, the job pool would be thick with applicants, but Adam hoped his qualifications at the

Wildlife Center would help carry him to the top of the pool.

"What about the Wildlife Center?"

"I will resign from the board," he said. "The board approved a new part-time director and with Angie and the volunteers, it should be staffed well."

"We are all so proud of you and how you worked so hard to build up the Wildlife Center. It's a real accomplishment to have the team of volunteers, funding, and support from not only Cranberry Bay but all the small towns in our county."

Adam nodded and ducked his head. He'd joined the Wildlife Center at the beginning of his sobriety five years ago. At the time he'd been trying to find his footing newly sober. The Wildlife Center needed someone to coordinate the volunteers who drove the hurt birds to the Center. Seagulls with broken wings who had been chased by dogs on the beach, common murres who failed to make their jumps from the large sea stacks, a few tufted puffins, and in the fall, pelicans. The pelicans were the most heartbreaking. They arrived in large tubs, the kind his mom used to store Christmas items, thrashing around, one wing bent in the wrong angle. All the birds came in with their feathers matted, unable to clean themselves.

Five years ago, the Wildlife Center had been a simple building with a few cages for the injured sea life and birds. He'd secured funding, created a non-profit with a board, and sought out some of the most influential people in the county to sit on the board. The Center occupied a sprawling five-acre property with numerous outdoor enclosures of all sizes for the injured birds, a floating pool for the common murre, and a large shower enclosure for the pelicans. He loved his work at the Wildlife Center and it fulfilled a need in him he hadn't known he had—the need to help.

He needed the Center as much as it needed him. He wished he could take the part-time director position. But this new job would allow him to continue to expand his work both in conservation and developing new programs. He would miss the shorebirds and the coastal waters he'd grown up around. He would miss his family and friends who made Cranberry Bay home. But he lost his job, and he was going to have to relocate somewhere to continue working with the environment and land that he loved.

"I'm planning to buy a home." He looked over at his mom. "A place for you to visit. A special room just for you. I won't have to be in a trailer anymore." Affordable housing in Cranberry Bay was practically non-existent just like it was all up and down the coast. One of the perks of his job was that he'd been living in a small trailer provided by the state parks. The property had been donated by a family who first settled the Oregon Coast and for generations it was maintained by the State Parks System as one of the crown jewels of the parks.

Rebecca smiled and said, "I just want you to be happy, my dear."

Adam picked up his mom's hand. He squeezed. "I know." His Mom had been his number one supporter throughout his sobriety. She attended family week when he was in treatment, attended Al-Anon meetings once a week, and worked hard to support him while not enabling him. He'd always been grateful to her. He'd seen other men and women in treatment who had no one supporting them. He knew alcoholism was a tough road and a lot of wives and families had had enough by the time their loved one got to sobriety. But he also knew what a difference a supportive family member could make and he never failed to tell his mom how much her support meant to him.

He drove through the rain and up the hill to his childhood home. Inside the front window, Sasha, Katie, and Rylee gathered around the large dining room table.

"Wedding planning," Rebecca said and smiled. "Sasha wants a 1950s style wedding and must have checked out every wedding book in the library system."

Adam was happy for his friends and brothers as each one got married. But it wasn't for him. He'd sworn off love. "I'm just glad it's not me," Adam said and shook his head. Sawyer and Katie's wedding had been lavish and Bryan and Rylee's small and intimate. A few months ago, his long-time best friend, Josh had married town antique shop owner, Ivy on Valentine's Day, and they announced a baby on the way soon after. And now, Sasha and Greg. He was the remaining bachelor of his brothers and best friend. Something he predicted would remain true since he just didn't think he'd be a good father or husband after the failed kayak accident. He'd proven himself unable to protect someone under his care.

"You gotta take it one day at a time," his AA sponsor, Seth, said. His own relationship with his high school crush, Suzanne, lit up Seth's life. But Adam's friendship with Gracie was enough.

"Coming in?" Rebecca asked.

Adam shook his head. "I need to get going and check on the park. There's a surfer who thinks he can sneak in for free without paying the park entrance fee. I've caught him twice and he always has some excuse for why he missed the box." Adam shook his head. "The surfers usually buy the park annual pass, but this guy seems to think the rules don't apply to him."

Even though his job had been terminated last week, he'd been allowed to continue to live in the trailer outside the park. Since there was not a replacement for his job, no one needed the trailer vacated. As long as he paid the electricity and water, he doubted anyone would send him packing. It'd been Adam's experience that the paperwork and bureaucracy in state and federal jobs often left many details unaccounted for, such as the small trailer housing. And he vowed that until he had another job, he would continue to protect the park he loved so much and that meant making sure that the entry fee was paid.

Rebecca leaned over and kissed her son's cheek. "I'm sure you'll take care of it. Thanks for the ride, dear. We'll see you later." She climbed out of the truck and went inside.

Adam turned the truck away from his home and toward the park. Fifteen minutes later, he pulled up the long, winding gravel road to the pay station. The park was between Seashore Cove and Cranberry Bay, just off the main highway that ran alongside the coast. A light rain pattered on his roof as he parked beside the trailer. The tall evergreens swayed in the breeze and a trail overlooked the sweeping coastline. The wide sandy beaches stretched for miles. A lone walker with her dog dotted the coast. Adam smiled. Even at this distance, he knew Gracie and her dog. Every evening at sunset, rain or shine, she drove the fifteen-minute trip from Cranberry Bay and strolled the wide-open beach while Max ran ahead of her.

Sometimes Rylee joined her with Raisin, but most of the time Gracie walked alone. It wasn't a well-used beach like the ones further down in the tourist towns of Seashore Cove. Adam often watched Gracie, just to make sure nothing happened. In the winter, the sneakier waves could wash ashore quickly and sweep someone and their dog out to sea with the logs that rolled in with the waves. Gracie was always careful and walked way above the shoreline, but he liked to watch, just in case with his cell phone close by in his pocket.

The first time he met Gracie on the trail, with her red hair in curly ringlets around her face, he'd felt himself entranced with the high-spirited independent woman. She'd taken up walking with him and was an easy conversationalist, well read, and interested in a wide array of naturalistic subjects. He enjoyed their walks on the trails. But Gracie was also guarded. She kept a part of her tucked away and at times, he'd catch the flash of pain across her face. It mirrored his own internal pain that sometimes he couldn't stop from coursing through him. Pain over the loss of the child in the kayak, pain over the wasted years of drinking when he'd tried to numb that pain, and so he didn't press her, unwilling to share his own.

As the spring and summer days moved to fall, he'd been happy to see the pain ease from her eyes as she made herself more and more part of the town and joined the group of passionate women who involved themselves in Cranberry Bay. Rylee, Katie, Sasha, and Ivy extended their friendship and small-town business sensibilities to Gracie as she built and established the inn. They enfolded her into small town life.

Adam leaned down and picked up a large stick. He had created a stick library for dogs on the trail and often gathered sticks to leave in the large glass enclosure he'd built.

He wasn't immune to heartache. Sometimes at night, he'd stare at the stars and remember how much he had given of himself to a woman who had been his best friend since kindergarten. He'd found himself her protector during the first week of school, when her lunch had been stolen and tossed all over the playground by the class bully. He had shared his own lunch that day, splitting his peanut butter and jelly sandwich carefully in half and opening his bag of Fritos. They had shared the homemade chocolate chip cookies.

But after the kayak accident and his descent into drinking, she'd left him, finding another man who she married. He knew he hadn't been the best man for her and made his amends after he got into AA. He was happy for her new life in Seashore Cove.

Adam stepped into the trailer. It didn't seem like the surfer was going to try and sneak in tonight. There had been one guy for the last year, an older heavy-set man, who constantly snuck in without paying first. When confronted, he always paid the fee and said he just forgot. Adam went along with the game, but he knew better.

He filled the coffee pot with water and scooped decaf coffee into a filter. He sat down at the table and opened his laptop. Glancing at the letter inside the envelope for the website address, he typed it in and an online application popped up with the city of Great Falls. He checked the box for the environmental center director. It was the only job available, and he reaffirmed to himself one of his favorite AA slogans: *Let Go and Let God.*

Chapter 4

"Room four is ready." Maddie dropped a large pile of towels and sheets into the laundry basket. "Who stayed in that room this weekend? It was a mess." Maddie wiped her hands on her black leggings. She wore a red t-shirt with Cranberry Bay High School written across the front in white letters. Her long, dark hair was held back in a clip as a few strands dangled around her face and neck.

"Annie and Betsy Sparks. They are sisters and return every year." Gracie enjoyed having eighteen-year-old Maddie around to help on weekends. It was busy trying to turn over the rooms. The hotel association suggested not to allow single night room rentals on weekends to make things easier, but that hadn't been possible in the small town. People usually didn't want two nights. They were passing through on the way to the bigger coastal towns and only needed one night.

Gracie had watched Maddie change from an angry,

hurt teenager when she'd first arrived in Cranberry Bay with her mom, Lisa, a few years ago, to a determined and focused teenager. For the last two years, she'd been part of the honor society at the high school and served on the student body government. Maddie's uncles, Bryan and Sawyer, had bets placed that she would choose one of their colleges to attend, University of Oregon or University of Washington.

Maddie opened the washing machine lid. "They made a mess. Sand and dirt everywhere, trash cans full of take-out, and empty soda cans on every surface."

"Good thing we have you to clean up!" Gracie said and smiled.

"Mmmmm…" Maddie turned the washer knob, and a stream of water poured out of the attached hose into the tub. "Maybe we should charge a surcharge!"

Gracie laughed. Maddie's keen sense of business would serve her well in her future career, whatever she chose to do.

Maddie's phone buzzed and she picked it up. Her face lit up and she texted a response.

"Lars?" Gracie picked up a yellow hand towel and folded it.

"Yes." Maddie tucked her phone into the side pocket of her leggings.

Maddie started dating Lars last Christmas during Photos with Santa at Paige's dog shop. She had been working at Ivy's antique shop for the holiday season, but Paige had convinced her they needed another hand for the photos with Santa dog shots. It hadn't taken much persuading when Maddie and Lars discovered their mutual interest in each other. They tried to keep their budding relationship private, but in a small town like Cranberry Bay, it was nearly impossible and by Valentine's Day, they were seen everywhere together. Gracie hoped both planned to attend the same college. It could be hard to keep a high school love strong if they went to different colleges. She had lost her own high school sweetheart in college when they attended universities on opposite ends of the state.

"He got his college acceptance," Maddie said, her voice unreadable. "University of Portland."

Gracie eyed Maddie as she placed a large bath towel in a stack. "That's not too far from the University of Oregon or the University of Washington. Weekend trips?"

"I guess." Maddie removed a washcloth from the dryer and folded it. She placed it on top of the pile of towels.

Gracie didn't want to pry. She knew the whole college choice was a stressful situation and with both of Maddie's uncles placing bets on which college she would choose, Gracie didn't want to upset her.

"I also got my acceptance," Maddie said, her voice quiet.

Gracie stopped folding and waited.

"I got into both the University of Oregon and the University of Washington."

"That's wonderful!" Gracie said. "Neither of your uncles will win the bet."

Maddie smiled but her smile didn't meet her eyes. "No, they won't."

Max trotted into the laundry room and pressed his snout against Maddie's hand, as if he knew she needed comfort. She knelt and wrapped her arms around the dog. Gracie's heart hurt for Maddie. She reminded her of a small child who needed comfort. A lot of comfort.

Gracie placed her hand on Maddie's shoulder and squeezed. "I know you'll make the choice that works best for you."

"I guess." Maddie didn't look up at her and held onto Max as if her life depended on it.

THAT AFTERNOON, Gracie slipped into the back of the crowd gathered in the marina shop. The run-down building had been transformed in the last four months. Wood beams crossed the ceiling as sunlight poured in from the large floor-to-ceiling windows. Racks of outdoor wear, including rain jackets, fleece and nylon shirts, and shorts, were placed along the left side of the store.

Rows of kayaks, solo and tandem, leaned along two sides of the building. Paddles, life jackets, and small wheeled carts for carrying the kayaks down to the river were neatly stacked on the floor. A large white board calendar announced new classes for beginners, women's only classes, and bird watching tours. A pocket of folded pamphlets with information on the classes, the spring schedule, and registration instructions, was placed in front of the whiteboard.

Suzanne had spared no expense when she decided to open the Cranberry Bay Marina Kayak Shop. She stood at the front of the room, wearing black nylon slacks, a zip up sports jacket, and waterproof boat shoes.

"It's about time to open, Suz," Seth said as he wiped down the counter behind her. Although Seth prided himself on staying off the grid, he'd been working with Suzanne for months on getting the shop ready. Gracie had seen the two of them paddling kayaks around the bay as the sun set, their kayaks drifting close together and gliding through the water. It'd been a surprise to everyone to find Suzanne and Seth rekindling their love last Christmas when Suzanne announced she was coming home to Cranberry Bay for good and leaving her swimming coaching job at the University of Washington. Seth had even been seen in the bakery with the locals for the morning coffee hour at Sasha's bakery, breaking his off-the-grid lifestyle and talking up the new marina kayak shop.

"I want to thank everyone," Suzanne said, her voice choked. "I couldn't have taken the steps toward this dream without the support of Cranberry Bay." She cleared her throat. Seth slipped out from behind the counter and stepped up beside her. He placed his hand on her lower back, a soft protective gesture that didn't go unnoticed by Gracie. What would it be like to have the support of someone who loved her as she reached toward her dreams? She had Adam's friendship and that was all she claimed she wanted.

But a small feeling of doubt played around the edges of her mind. Was that really all she wanted? Sometimes she could feel a desire for more bubbling under the surface, but she quickly pushed it away, denying any feelings beyond friendship. Would she ever feel strongly enough to take the risk to fall in love again?

"I'm signing up for the women's class." Rylee stepped forward and raised her phone to the QR code on the whiteboard.

"Me too!" Sasha turned to Greg. "I want to get Tyler signed up, too. What do you think?'

Greg whipped out his phone and clicked on the QR code. "Done."

Sasha smiled and leaned up on her tiptoes to kiss Greg. The two of them made no secret of the love they felt for each other and their ten-year-old son.

The room erupted in cheers. Sasha and Greg's romance had been a town favorite last Christmas as everyone watched the two former college sweethearts as they came together and formed a family with their son, Tyler. Tyler had finally learned to swim and was often seen with Greg on his sailboat. Greg had pledged to buy a set of small single sail sailboats and would teach a class for kids in the summer as part of the new marina shop.

"I'd like to try the bird watching tour." Gracie loved watching the songbirds and hoped to encourage more birds to visit her yard this spring with new feeders in the inn's backyard, even if that backyard was a little overgrown. The birds wouldn't mind and she would enjoy watching them from her kitchen window. Plus, a couple of the upstairs rooms that overlooked the backyard would also have views of the birds and feeders.

The crowd drifted throughout the kayak shop, combing through the racks of clothing. Seth explained the difference between a couple of the kayaks to Sawyer, Bryan, and Josh.

Gracie didn't bother to look around the room for Adam. She knew he wouldn't be here. She hadn't lived in Cranberry Bay when the kayak accident happened, and Adam didn't talk about it. But Cranberry Bay was a small town, and everyone knew Adam had failed a water rescue one summer and lost a child. That child had been the niece of his long-time high school girlfriend who everyone had assumed Adam would marry. But the accident had broken up the relationship and she married someone else.

"Gracie?" Sasha touched her arm. "Everything okay?"

"Sure." Gracie turned and smiled at Sasha.

"I don't know." Sasha shook her head. "You had a very faraway look on your face."

"I was just thinking," Gracie said.

"Adam?" Sasha said.

The flush and heat rose in Gracie's face.

"It's okay," Sasha said. "I don't think anyone expected him to be here."

"I guess not," Gracie said. "Maybe I was just hoping he would come. It seems strange to be at a Cranberry

Bay event and not have him here." Adam attended every Cranberry Bay festival and activity, from the July 4th Festivities in the park, to the Christmas tree lighting, to the Halloween trick-or-treating downtown. He was always willing to help whenever someone needed him.

"Did you get a chance to look at the new jackets?" Sasha pointed to the row of all-weather proof jackets hanging on a small post. "I'm going to get one. Greg wants to go out on the sailboat more now that the weather is turning nicer."

Gracie followed Sasha and the two worked their way through the racks. She was happy to see Sasha finally able to purchase things she wanted for herself. For as long as Gracie had known her, Sasha worked hard to keep her bakery afloat and raise Tyler as a single mom. But all that had changed with Greg. Determined not to let him buy her or her love, Sasha had maintained her stance of remaining independent as the two had fallen in love. As her love for Greg bloomed and she recognized that he was expressing his feelings for her by being able to share his prosperity and success with her.

Sasha lifted a jacket from a hanger. She slipped her arms into the blue jacket. The color highlighted her sparkling eyes, and she zipped it up around her petite frame. "I'm really nervous about the wedding."

"You are? Do you want to talk about it?" Gracie pointed to the small porch overlooking the river.

Sasha nodded and followed Gracie outside the double wide glass sliding doors and onto a wooden deck. They walked over to two green Adirondack chairs at the edge of the deck, overlooking the water. Gracie sat down in one and Sasha sat in the other, but she didn't sit back in the chair, she perched on the edge.

"Is everything okay?" Gracie asked. She hoped Sasha wasn't afraid about the wedding. Sometimes weddings could be overwhelming. Her own was supposed to be a three-hundred-person wedding. Something she never would have agreed to if she had known it would be called off days before.

"I'm not nervous about marrying Greg, I love him with all my heart. But I don't want a big wedding." Sasha swallowed. "I just want it to be a small private event with my closest friends."

"I understand," Gracie said, nodding. She knew that if she ever even considered marriage again, which she wasn't planning to, she would never do a large three-hundred-person wedding. It had been devastating to tell all the invited guests there was no wedding three days before it was to take place. The well-meaning questions and comments had unsettled her and spiked her anxiety. Her ex-fiancé, Mike, had smoothly suggested that some of the reservations, such as the food catering, could simply be rescheduled for his wedding to Amy. Devastated and filled with sadness and disbelief, Gracie had agreed, asking only that her reservations for the honeymoon on the Oregon Coast not be canceled. Of course, once she'd arrived in Cranberry Bay and found the inn, she'd canceled the rest of their hotel reservations and allowed the late penalties to be charged to his accounts.

"I know everyone expects to be invited," Sasha said,

and smiled. "And I would love to have a reception where we can invite everyone in town. But, I was wondering…" Sasha trailed off.

Gracie leaned closer to Sasha. She knew that Sasha was outgoing and friendly, and it served her well in her bakery but underneath that, Sasha was very private. She'd learned to accept help from her friends in Cranberry Bay when she needed support with Tyler, but she'd do whatever she could to make sure she didn't gather a lot of debts from her friends, and made sure to always offer free coffee, sandwiches, and baked goods whenever she could.

"On the house," she would say and wink as she handed a bag filled with chocolate chip scones or raspberry scones to someone.

"Do you think we could have the wedding at your inn?" Sasha asked and swallowed. "It's a small venue and that way I wouldn't have to explain why we are not having a large wedding. We can still have the reception at Katie and Sawyer's place."

"The inn?" Gracie frowned. The inn's small living room barely held her piano, a sideboard where she served tea and cookies, and a small couch set.

"Yes," Sasha said. "It's cozy and warm. Unless you don't want…."

"Of course we can have it at the inn." She would make it work for Sasha. She would do whatever she needed to do, move furniture, even move the piano if needed.

"Thank you." The cloud from Sasha's face cleared

and she stood. "Do you think I should pay for this jacket?" Sasha said and laughed. "I don't want to take it off."

Gracie followed Sasha into the marina shop. A small quiver of doubt played at her mind. She wanted to host the wedding for Sasha. But where would they host it? And more importantly, how much of her own painful memories would she have to face by being so close to her friend's wedding?

Chapter 5

Adam folded the last chair and slid it into the church closet behind the large box with the coffee pot. He placed the stack of AA literature on the shelf above the coffee pot. The meeting tonight had been small, but those were often better meetings because people could share their stories for longer periods of time. He didn't usually attend an AA meeting on Sunday nights, but he needed to get out of Cranberry Bay. The last place he wanted to be was the marina shop open house. When he told Seth, he'd shaken his head and given him one of those looks, the ones that said he wasn't being honest.

"You are going to need to face this," he'd said. "AA Meetings are important, but they aren't meant for hiding places."

But Adam hadn't wanted to face the painful memories, not yet. Maybe never. He was happy that Suzanne was bringing a marina shop to Cranberry Bay and hoped it would bring in more people who would stop for a day trip to kayak or rent one of the small sailboats Greg was planning to purchase. But he didn't need to be involved in this new endeavor, especially since he would leave for a new job soon.

He'd finished his application last night and found a couple more jobs to apply for—one in Michigan that looked like a long shot due to the requirements in the application, and another one in upstate New York which would take him across the country and severely limit the amount of time he could see his family and friends. He was hoping to get the Montana job since that didn't seem so far from Cranberry Bay and it seemed the most interesting to him.

After he finished putting everything away, Adam slipped out the back doors of the church. A couple men hung around, chatting. He nodded to them, not wanting to linger tonight and got into his truck. In fifteen minutes, he was pulling into Cranberry Bay. He drove down Main Street. Gracie stood outside the inn, a large bag of soil beside her and a carton of geraniums and petunias on the sidewalk.

The evening sun cast shadows alongside the stone wall of the two-story brick inn. In winter, the darkness would have descended but in spring and summer, the evening hours stretched well past nine PM. There was plenty of time to plant flowers in the pots alongside the front door.

Adam slowed and pulled into one of the parking spots parallel to the inn. The inn had a handful of spots in the back, close to the door leading up the staircase to the second-floor rooms. Adam knew not to park in any of those spots, even if they were empty. Parking was limited in Cranberry Bay and each business guarded their spots with signs, cones, and even roped off areas. Although there were a couple empty spots, a guest could be eating in Seashore Cove and arrive back to find all the parking spaces gone. It could quickly spiral into negative reviews on the travel sites. Adam got out and headed toward Gracie. She knelt on a small blue mat and bent over a large mosaic pot.

"Need some help?" he asked.

Gracie looked up and a smile lit across her face. "Sure!"

Adam hefted one of the large bags of soil lying on the ground. He positioned himself in front of the pot and angled the bag so the soil wouldn't land on the sidewalk. Any day now, the city would place hanging baskets along the streetlamp on big S hooks. Big baskets overflowing with colorful petunias. The baskets were new, part of a city program purchased with funds from the new lodging and tourism tax. The tax wasn't as high as the beach towns lodging tax, and there were only a handful of bed and breakfasts, Gracie's inn and Rylee's cottages, but every little bit counted and made a difference in what Cranberry Bay could do to attract tourists as they drove through the town on their way to the beach towns. Cranberry Bay often seemed like an afterthought for most people, but the Council and Chamber of Commerce had been working hard to bring more tourists with festivals and now Suzanne's kayak tours.

Adam finished filling the pots with soil. Gracie lifted purple and white petunias from small containers and placed them into the soil. By the end of June, the pots would be bursting with color. The peace of the early evening settled over Adam as he enjoyed the companionship with Gracie, which always lifted his heart.

It'd been a shock to lose his job with the parks department. The country seemed to be in an uproar over budget cuts to parks in every state. He knew he would have to hustle to find a new job. The competition would be fierce with so many people out of work. The last few days, he'd been so focused on searching and applying for jobs that he had forgotten to take time to relax.

"How are the wedding plans going?" Adam asked and smiled. He knew Gracie felt the same way he did about weddings. They were great for other people, but not for themselves. They'd had multiple conversations about their friends and the frequent weddings happening in Cranberry Bay, and both always emphasized they weren't looking for a wedding themselves.

"Sasha wants to have the wedding at the inn," Gracie said as she stood and straightened. She rubbed her lower back. "I told her we could make it work. It's just going to be about fifteen or so people."

A hummingbird darted above Adam's head and fluttered away. "That's a change. What happened to Katie and Sawyer's barn?"

Katie and Sawyer's barn wasn't a barn, it was a barn

that had been turned into an elegant building with heat, water, and floors where Katie hosted sewing classes and occasionally rented it out for events.

"She still wants the reception to be at the barn. She's just asking for the ceremony to be more private."

"What about the backyard?" Adam nodded toward the wrought iron gate leading to the backyard behind the inn. He'd fixed the latch a couple times over the last few months and encouraged Gracie to slip a small lock on it if she didn't want local teens exploring in places they shouldn't be.

"The backyard is full of blackberry bushes and weeds. I don't even know how much work it would take to make it wedding worthy in such a short time."

"That's just how it looks right now," Adam hummed. There was nothing more that he loved than clearing out an area that had become overgrown with weeds and creating a new space. "But we could fix that." The opportunity to work with Gracie to shape the backyard into a garden oasis seemed perfect. It would give him something to do while he waited to hear back about his job applications. And it was a chance to spend time with Gracie which he enjoyed a lot. Neither one of them wanted to fall in love. They were two friends, working together to create a shared wedding space. It seemed ideal.

Gracie slipped off her garden gloves and placed them in a small bucket. "A functional backyard would give the inn an additional selling point. We could host garden parties and small events. I would love to plant flowers and bushes that will attract more birds."

Adam shifted, the way he often did when something excited him as if he couldn't keep his enthusiasm trapped in his body. "I know just the right combination. We could even get the backyard certified as a natural habitat. Let's go take a look."

Gracie picked up the bucket with her shovel, gloves, and small rake. Adam hoisted the half-empty bag of soil and followed Gracie through the gate into the backyard.

A gazebo sat on the far end of the garden. It'd become overgrown with blackberry bushes and weeds. What was once a gravel path had tall weeds, and black-berries grew alongside the back fence creating a thick wall.

"There is so much to do." Gracie waved her hand over the garden. "The gazebo is going to need some repair and a new coat of paint. We'll need an area for chairs. I'd like to see at least one pond and, of course, blooming flowers and plants." She bit her lower lip. "I really want to do this for Sasha, but it's going to be a push."

"We can do it." Adam eyed the backyard. His mind raced with a list of possibilities. Even with the wedding only a few weeks away, it would be possible to get the yard cleared out and new plants planted. They could purchase plants from a nursery in Portland that special-ized in full grown bushes, shrubs, and trees.

"There are stone walkways under the overgrown grass. If we can get the tall grasses and weeds cleared away, we might be able to find some of them." She had never seen the backyard in its full glory, but she saw pictures in a photo album tucked away in the attic of the inn. At one point, someone had loved gardening and created a peaceful sanctuary.

"Not a problem," Adam said. "I can take care of that in a couple days with the right tools and equipment. What else?"

"We could have the chairs over there." Gracie pointed at the grass in front of the gazebo. "Grass is just not practical on the coast. It's too rainy and I don't want to put down chemicals."

"That sounds doable." Adam surveyed the yard.

Gracie brushed the hair off her forehead. "I don't know. It's a lot of work. But it's Sasha. And I want to do this for her."

"We can do it," Adam said. He smiled at Gracie and held out his hand to shake hers.

She slipped her hand into his and a small spark fired inside him. He quickly pushed it down as his phone buzzed in his back pocket with the alert of a text. He dropped Gracie's hand and pulled his phone out of his back pocket.

We'd like to set up an interview. Please call us.

Adam couldn't stop the grin.

"Good news?" Gracie asked.

Adam pocketed his phone. "I got a job interview."

"That's great," Gracie said, and smiled. "Where?"

"In Great Falls, Montana."

Chapter 6

"Aunt Celia?" Gracie knocked on the door to her bedroom. She rubbed her lower back. The pull-out couch in the living room of her suite of rooms wasn't the best bed but she wanted her aunt to have her room. "We're running a little late. Are you ready?" The last thing she wanted to be was late for the Shuster Sunday brunch. She usually helped Katie set the table and cut up the fruit for the fruit tray. The fruit varied by season and although it was still a little early for strawberries, she knew Katie would pull out strawberries and raspberries she'd frozen.

The bright sunshine shone through the high windows and along the hallway carpet. Gracie stopped to straighten tulips in a simple glass canning container on an old dresser tucked into a small alcove. The dresser was perfect for storing towels and sheets for the rooms on the second floor and had been a find in Ivy's antique shop.

"I'm ready, dear." Aunt Celia opened her bedroom

door. She wore a long, flowing green and white skirt, a white top, and a colorful scarf filled with dainty flowers. Gold hoop earrings hung from her ears and a diamond bracelet on her left wrist.

"You look nice." Gracie bit her lower lip. She'd told Aunt Celia the brunch was casual. But she hadn't listened which wasn't unusual. Her aunt always did what she wanted, and her mom often claimed it was why Aunt Celia never found one person to settle down with after she divorced her first husband.

Aunt Celia usually brushed the complaints aside and said her first husband had left her with enough money to do whatever she wanted anyway and that was what she got for putting up with him for ten years. Gracie had never known her uncle. Celia had married young, and he'd worked as a financial broker in Chicago. She often talked about the lifestyle they led—trips to the Caribbean in the winter, and summers in the Hamptons. It sounded so fancy to Gracie. But Aunt Celia always said, *"Appearances are not what they seem, dear."*

After they divorced, Celia moved back to St. Louis and lived in a large sprawling home with a pool in Ladue. She hired the best divorce lawyer she could and got quite the settlement.

Gracie had loved spending the hot, humid summer St. Louis days in her aunt's pool, and Celia loved filling her home with people and parties. As a big movie fan, she always hosted the Oscar and Academy Award parties where guests dressed up in formal wear. Her aunt loved dressing up in all kinds of clothes and costumes. At

Mardi Gras, she was the first to arrive at the big St. Louis parties and spent long evenings moving among masked guests.

Gracie didn't want her aunt to feel uncomfortable at the Shuster brunch when everyone else would be in jeans.

"I can't wait to meet Rebecca Shuster," Aunt Celia said. "I hope we can spend more time together." She turned back to her dressing table and slipped another three bracelets on her right wrist. They clanked together as she picked up a colorful sun hat hanging on a small hook next to the bathroom door. "I'd like to get to know people in Cranberry Bay. It seems like a wonderful town, and I'd like to stay for a while."

Gracie headed down the stairs, doubts fluttering in her mind. Usually, her aunt visited for only a week. Gracie couldn't imagine her aunt living in Cranberry Bay for an extended time. She thrived too much on her busy obligations and social life in St. Louis. A social life that didn't exist in Cranberry Bay. Gracie didn't want to hurt her aunt, but Rebecca Shuster and Aunt Celia were two very different women. Rebecca was quiet and reserved. She rarely joined in the town's events, preferring to keep to herself, reading or working on her embroidery.

She'd given Gracie a beautiful embroidery sampler for the inn, which hung in the living room. Many guests commented on the beautiful stitching. Gracie also loved embroidery herself and made a few dish towels, which of course could not be used due to the delicate stitching. They hung on small hooks in the kitchen. Her favorite was a towel with a small white dog and a ball.

When Gracie reached the bottom of the steps, she flipped the small hand-painted sign hanging on a hook on the back of the front door to *Gone for Lunch.* She'd be back in a couple hours. Everyone who needed to check out had already left, and there were no new reservations for tonight. Flipping the lock on the front door, Gracie turned around expecting to see her aunt behind her. Aunt Celia gestured and her voice raised as she talked to someone on her cell phone.

Suddenly Aunt Celia clicked off her phone and dropped it into her bag. She hurried down the stairs and didn't say a word to Gracie about the phone call. Instead, she followed her to the side door leading out to the small parking lot behind the inn. A black wrought iron fence dived the parking from the backyard.

Once in the car and her aunt settled in the passenger seat, Gracie slipped on her sunglasses. She wanted to say something about the phone call but knew enough not to pry. Aunt Celia would tell her when she was ready. Gracie turned out of town and headed toward Katie and Sawyer's home. The Shuster Sunday brunches had expanded so much that Rebecca turned it over to be hosted at Katie and Sawyer's home. Their large kitchen had beautiful appliances and cookware. The table, which seated twelve, worked much better than the cozy kitchen and dining area in Rebecca's craftsman home. Especially as spring warmed up and they could sprawl out on the spacious patio.

"Tell me everything about Adam." Aunt Celia settled her large bag on her lap and dug for her sunglasses. She pulled out a purple and gold pair with heart-shaped eyes and sparkles on the edges and.

Gracie flushed. She needed to set Aunt Celia straight about her friendship with Adam.

"Adam is my friend," Gracie said. "We hike together, and sometimes I drive the injured sea birds to the Wildlife Center."

"A friend that you have feelings for." Aunt Celia patted her leg.

"No," Gracie said, her voice strong and firm. Aunt Celia had supported her during her relationship with Mike. She'd seen the bruises after Gracie confessed that Mike hit her when he got angry. Aunt Celia had offered her a place to stay on nights when Gracie was afraid Mike would return home drunk and belligerent. Gracie knew it was a mistake to move in with Mike before they were married, but he'd convinced her with his charm and by buying a home she'd loved as soon as it came on the market.

"It will be our early wedding present," he'd told her. She believed him and moved in which had only made her worry more about his drinking problem and heightened the threat of abuse after too many drinks.

"Adam and I are friends." Gracie hit the gas pedal hard, and the car picked up the required speed on the highway leading out of town. "He's applying for jobs and has a job interview in Montana."

"Montana is a nice place to live." Aunt Celia rolled down her window. She clutched her sun hat and turned her face to the sun.

"I guess." Gracie slowed the car and turned into Sawyer and Katie's long driveway. She could never leave Cranberry Bay, the inn, and her friendships.

Aunt Celia dangled her fingers from the car. "This is a beautiful spot."

Gracie pulled alongside Adam's black truck. "It is," she said, relieved to have the focus shifted away from her and Adam. "Sawyer was so happy when Katie agreed to marry him. He felt terrible that her quilt shop went out of business because of the large superstore he brought to the outskirts of Cranberry Bay." She put the car in park. Aunt Celia opened her door and stepped out.

Gracie tried to gather her feelings. Her heart beat fast with nerves. She hoped Aunt Celia didn't continue with her ideas about Adam. She was known for blurting out whatever she was thinking or feeling and the last thing Gracie needed was Aunt Celia to mention her romantic ideas about her and Adam to everyone, especially in front of Adam.

Aunt Celia stepped beside her. She adjusted her sun hat against a small breeze and placed her sunglasses on. "I hope you find the same, my dear." Aunt Celia opened her arms and hugged her.

Gracie hugged her aunt back and felt how frail she had become. Was something wrong with her aunt? Was she sick? Her aunt had never been one to diet or work on losing weight. She always kept herself fit and ate well-balanced meals. Before she could express her concern, her aunt whispered against her cheek. "You deserve to have someone who loves you, too."

Gracie doubted she would ever be able to trust in loving someone again. Not after what had happened with Mike. The best she could hope for was a nice friendship like the one she had with Adam. But it didn't hurt to allow Aunt Celia to have her romantic fantasies of a happily ever after. Her aunt had spent a lot of nights worrying about Gracie when she was with Mike.

"Gracie!" Katie opened the side door of her home, which led to a paved porch filled with patio furniture, a large table, and two gas grills. She carried a tray of fruit. "It's such a nice afternoon. Sawyer is grilling salmon, and Rylee is working on eggs and scones."

Gracie hurried over to Katie. Aunt Celia walked behind her, her high heels sinking in the wet grass. Spring on the coast was wet, there was no way getting around it. Gracie loved her sports and hiking shoes. Today she'd chosen her tennis shoes to go with a pair of jeans and a long sleeve blue shirt she wore under a zip up jacket. She'd pulled her hair back with a colorful headband and wore only a small pair of earrings made by a local artist.

She loved attending the summer market and supporting the local jewelry artists by purchasing bracelets and earrings. The simple jewelry was perfect.

"It's so wet," Aunt Celia said. Her heel slipped into the wet ground again. She reached out and grabbed Gracie's arm.

"We should get you a pair of good tennis shoes," Gracie said. "You'll need them for a few more weeks before the rains stop for the summer." She also didn't want her aunt to fall and break a bone, especially if she was already struggling with a health issue.

"Where are Sasha and Greg?" Gracie asked as she hugged Katie. Sasha usually made sure to stack the Sunday brunches with the best croissants and scones from the bakery.

"They took the sailboat out with Tyler." Katie's eyes sparkled above a colorful green and yellow scarf she'd looped loosely around her neck. She wore jeans and a white blouse with a simple pair of gold earrings and a matching teardrop necklace. Katie always managed to look effortless in her simple elegance, a trait Sawyer always complimented her on.

Gracie followed Katie to the side patio. Suzanne stood behind Seth and massaged his neck.

"He lifted too many kayaks," she said, and smiled at Gracie. Suzanne wore black nylon stretch pants and an oversized sweatshirt with the name and logo of the kayak shop. Seth wore a matching sweatshirt and jeans. Suzanne and Seth became regular attendees of the Sunday brunch over the last couple months. The two fit easily into the ease of the friendship and family group, despite Seth's initial grumbling about not wanting to spoil his image as the off-grid man of Cranberry Bay.

"How were the sales at the Kayak Shop opening?" Gracie asked Suzanne.

"Fabulous," Suzanne said. "We had a record number of people sign up for classes and more than a few people bought new kayaks."

"Anyone ready for a scone?" Rylee carried a plate of

scones and Ivy followed behind her with a small tray of jams and butter. Both wore jeans and colorful long sleeve blouses. Ivy had tied a simple red scarf around her neck. On the patio, Josh sat in a lounge chair. His and Ivy's six-month-old lay against his chest, sleeping. His fleece jacket was unzipped, and the baby nestled inside against his neck. Bryan and Greg stood at the grill, both wearing jeans and sweatshirts. Adam poured orange juice into glass cups on the table, his work boots sticking out of his dark blue jeans and a green parks long sleeved shirt.

"I think we're about ready." Rebecca Shuster walked out carrying a large bowl of scrambled eggs and placed it on the table. She also wore jeans and a colorful blouse. And like Gracie, she enjoyed the local artist jewelry and wore a pair of beaded earrings and matching bracelet on her wrist. The table had been set with white plates with small rings of spring flowers around them. Colorful glasses in pinks, greens, and blues sat at each setting.

Katie placed a couple bouquets of daffodils in glass jars as centerpieces. Katie loved combing through Ivy's antique shop for dishes. With her large kitchen and cabinets, she had plenty of room to store china and dishes others had discarded.

Gracie flushed. She and Aunt Celia had taken so long that she hadn't been able to help with the cooking or setting the table, something she loved to help with at the brunches. "I'm sorry we're late."

"It was all my fault," Aunt Celia said. "I just couldn't decide what to wear!" She eyed the table. "Where should I sit?"

"I'm sorry," Katie said. "I didn't realize we were having another guest. I'll grab another place setting."

A pit of anxiety formed in the middle of her stomach. Not only was she late, but she also hadn't told anyone that Aunt Celia was coming which wasn't usual for her. But she hadn't known Aunt Celia wanted to go until this morning when she announced that of course she wanted to attend the brunch. And while getting ready to go, it slipped her mind that she hadn't texted Katie to let her know to add another place setting.

"Let me help you." Gracie hurried behind Katie and into the large kitchen. Rylee followed behind with the empty tray.

"Everything okay?" Rylee asked as they stepped into the kitchen. Rylee was usually the first of the sewing circle women to spot that something was wrong. She called it her hypervigilance from growing up with her dad and his gambling addiction. Gracie shared that hypervigilance and anxiety but unlike Rylee, she kept her observations and fears to herself.

"Sure," Gracie said. She smiled the practiced smile she knew that covered everything when she didn't want people to know something was wrong. But she also knew she could trust Rylee if she shared her concerns about Aunt Celia. "Aunt Celia is going to stay in Cranberry Bay for a while. She is hoping she can become friends with Rebecca." Gracie lowered her voice. "I'm not sure why Aunt Celia wants to stay. I didn't know she was coming, and I think something may be wrong."

"Of course I'd like to get to know your aunt,"

Rebecca Shuster said as she stepped into the kitchen. She pulled open the utensil drawer. "There is a spring tea at the library coming up with a local author. Perhaps she'd like to attend that?"

Gracie reddened. She hoped Rebecca hadn't heard the part about her worries about her aunt. She didn't know if anything was wrong with her aunt, and she didn't want to worry her friends.

"That would be great but I don't know if she drinks tea." Gracie had never seen her aunt drink tea, and she didn't like to read. She loved her movies and TV shows that she could stream for hours. But maybe she would enjoy helping out and getting to know other people in Cranberry Bay. The library had a nice group who worked hard to bring authors to town, sponsored events such as the Read with a Dog, and held monthly meetings.

"The salmon is ready," Sawyer called, his voice loud and booming.

Rylee touched Gracie's hand. "Are you sure everything is okay and it's not just your aunt? You haven't said hello to Adam and the two of you are usually inseparable at brunch."

"Yes," Gracie said. She hadn't meant to ignore Adam, but a part of her wondered if she was protecting herself. Protecting herself from getting too close to him when he was applying for jobs in other states. Plus, she didn't want to draw attention to herself and Adam for fear of Aunt Celia saying something that would embarrass her and expose romantic dreams that just didn't exist.

Bryan stuck his head into the side door. "Food is getting cold," he said and smiled at Rylee.

Rylee lit up. She walked toward him and placed a small kiss on his cheek. "You know how much I love you."

Bryan wrapped Rylee in a big hug and placed a protective kiss on her head. "I do."

Gracie's insides warmed. It was so good to see people who loved and cared about each other. Even if it was something she could never see for herself, she liked knowing it existed.

Gracie followed Rylee to the patio. She sat down at the table beside her aunt and Maddie on the other side of her. Maddie turned and smiled at her. She poured orange juice from a small carton into a small glass and handed it to Gracie. "No pulp."

Gracie smiled at Maddie. Both of them detested pulp in their juice and always made sure to watch out for the other by not filling their glasses from the pulp juice pitcher. She still hadn't made eye contact with Adam and busied herself with taking a long drink of her juice.

Once everyone was seated and their plates were filled with salmon, scrambled eggs, and scones, Adam tapped the edge of his glass. "I have an announcement," he said.

Gracie's pulse quickened. She knew Adam would announce his job opportunity. She was happy for him, but a small part of her felt sad. Sad at losing her friend if he got the job.

The table quieted.

"I have an interview for a job in Montana,"

"That's wonderful!" Sawyer said and clapped. "What's the job?"

"It's for an executive director in a new city environmental and education center. I would love to stay in Cranberry Bay, but the job opportunities just aren't here."

The questions flew around the table about when the interview would take place and when he might find out if he got the job.

Gracie put a heaping spoonful of eggs into her mouth. She didn't raise her eyes to meet Adam's gaze. Beside her Maddie chewed her eggs as if her life depended on it. Gracie suspected the girl didn't want to bring attention to herself for fear someone might ask her about her college choices.

Rylee nudged her. "That's why you were quiet."

"Yes," Gracie said and turned to Rylee. "I didn't want to spoil the surprise."

"Will you be here for Sasha and Greg's wedding?" Katie asked as she forked a small piece of salmon.

"I wouldn't miss it," Adam said. "Gracie and I are working on fixing up the inn's garden."

"Sasha asked me to host the wedding at the inn," Gracie said, and smiled at Adam. "It's so wonderful that Adam is going to help me get it ready."

"That's fabulous!" Katie clapped her hands together. "It's a great opportunity for the inn and I know with the two of you working together, it will come together beautifully."

Feeling his gaze on her, Gracie raised her head and

looked into Adam's eyes. Her heart beat faster. Something inside her shifted as she looked at him. Where had these feelings come from? Was it because he might leave? She shook herself. She was practical. She had an inn to run, and friends who felt like family. She'd made a home for herself in Cranberry Bay. Adam was her friend. Nothing more. But why did she feel like something inside her had moved in a way she didn't expect.

Beside her, Maddie shifted and her arm brushed against Gracie. Gracie looked at Maddie and an exchange passed between them. An exchange that could only be identified as Maddie wasn't the only one with a conflicted secret she didn't want to voice today.

Chapter 7

Adam parked his truck alongside the back fence leading into the garden. He hopped out and pulled down the tailgate. He had piled the back of the truck with as many pieces of equipment as he thought they might need for clearing out the yard. He grabbed the large wheelbarrow and hoisted it from the truck bed.

"Looks like a project!" Josh pulled his bike next to Adam's truck. "Anything I can do to help?" He wore a nylon red jacket and black biking shorts. He loved to ride his bike and the early spring rides had already tanned his face.

"I'd love some help getting everything to the backyard," Adam said.

"Looks like you cleared out the parks department," Josh said, as he climbed off his bike. He parked it against the side of the truck and lifted a large weed trimmer and brush cutter out of the truck. Oregon State Parks was stamped across the handle.

"Unfortunately, visitors are going to see a lot of overgrown trails this summer." Adam shook his head. "Too many layoffs."

"Cranberry Bay will do what they can to help out." Josh pulled out a couple of rakes and a large shovel.

"Cranberry Bay, Seashore Cove, Pelican Shores," Adam said, listing all the small towns along the north coast. "We've got a good group of folks who volunteer. It's the other places, the smaller places or the loved too much places I'm worried about." He frowned. 'Loved too much' was a phrase a lot of the national parks and popular outdoor spots were calling it when too many tourists descended and the wear and tear on the places took a toll.

Places like Multnomah Falls outside of Portland were trying to control the problem by restricting parking to a certain number of slots in high volume traffic times. Sea Shore Cove City Council had discussed a few different ideas for paid parking, but the shops and restaurants filled the chamber for public comment, concerned that paid parking would limit the amount people wanted to spend for meals and gift items.

Josh dropped a couple bags of soil and compost into the wheelbarrow. "Heard anything more about your job applications?"

"Just the interview." Adam hopped into the back of the truck and grabbed a large tub. Cranberry Bay didn't have a yard waste pickup. Everything went over to the recycling center south of Sea Shore Cove. Adam enjoyed spending afternoons after he'd dropped off a truckload of grass cuttings, clippings, and weeds, poking through the recycled items in the reuse store. He'd found everything from an old-time radio to a record player to a handful of kitchen gadgets.

"You'll get it," Josh said. "I can't see how someone wouldn't hire you!"

"I think that's everything." Adam surveyed the pile of equipment and yard tools beside the truck and in the wheelbarrow. He always had a hard time taking compliments. Something deep inside him always felt like he didn't quite deserve the praise. Seth told him it had to do with the guilt he harbored over the kayak accident, and he needed to learn to forgive himself.

"Got it!" Josh picked up the rakes, shovel, and the large tub and headed toward the back gate.

Adam threw everything else into the wheelbarrow and walked behind him. "The gate is a little tricky." Adam stepped around Josh. He reached his hand over the gate and lifted the latch from the other side. He gave the gate a hard shove. "The weather warped the gate boards."

"I'll see if Bryan and I can get over here and fix it," Josh said. "He's been working on a couple of the river cottages and bought some new tools for grinding wood." Josh grinned. "I think he really wants to open a place for woodworking but hasn't convinced Rylee to go along with it, yet."

Adam nudged the gate open. He had no doubt Bryan would convince Rylee. He'd been in love with her since they were in high school and had been devastated when Rylee moved away. Watching Bryan fall in love with Rylee all over again when she moved back to Cranberry Bay to clean out her grandmother's home had been one of the highlights during his dark slide into alcoholism after the kayak accident. Even though he'd never trust himself again to protect someone close to him and be in love, he was happy to see his brother's long held dream come true.

In the backyard, Gracie pulled a thick ivy vine from alongside a tall tree. She wore heavy work gloves, jeans, and a blue sweatshirt. She'd put a baseball cap over her hair, but a ponytail stuck out the back.

"I got it." Adam stepped around Gracie and grabbed the vine. He gave a tug, and it fell off the tree. "You have to know where to pull the vine."

He dropped it into the large tub.

Gracie placed her hands on her hips and surveyed the yard. "It's a lot of work. I don't know if we can really have this ready in time."

"Sure we can," Adam said, optimism filling his chest.

Josh's cell buzzed. "I gotta get going," Josh said. "Ivy needs me to watch Izzy while she runs some errands."

"We've got it covered," Adam said, and gave Josh a shoulder hug. "Thanks for helping me get the stuff into the backyard."

"Where should we start?" Gracie waved her arms

around the yard. "I've pulled off some ivy, yanked out a few weeds, and uncovered a few stones. But I don't feel like I've gotten anywhere."

Adam's logical mind segmented the yard into quadrants. It was just a matter of uncovering each part piece by piece. People got overwhelmed with gardens and yards because they tried to do too much at once. He reached into his pocket and pulled out a small spiral notebook and a pen.

"Let's draw up a map. We'll divide the garden into segmented spots."

In minutes, he had the yard sectioned off on the paper with small notes for each section. "The first thing we want to do," Adam said, "is see what's under all this overgrown grass." He walked to the weed trimmer and put in a new spool of nylon thread. In one motion, he had the weed trimmer running with a loud purr. He walked along the garden edges, trimming back overgrown grasses and weeds. Small pieces of dirt and rock flew up and around him.

"Do you need eye goggles?" Gracie asked, her voice loud above the weed trimmer.

Adam opened his mouth to answer at the same time as a small rock slipped from under the weed trimmer and sliced the edges of his hand. He clicked the button to off, released the weed trimmer, and dropped it to the ground.

"Adam!" Gracie hurried over to him.

He wrapped his hand in his flannel sleeve and tried to smile. "It's okay."

"It's not okay." Gracie took his hand. "We need to get

this washed off and dressed. I have a first aid kit in the kitchen."

Adam followed Gracie into the house. He'd been hurt before—things happened. He had the scars to prove it on his arms and legs. But something inside him felt soft and warm at Gracie's touch and concern.

In the kitchen, Gracie pulled out a chair at the table and he lowered himself into it. He placed his hand on the table, making sure to keep the flannel covering his hand. But the blood crept through the flannel shirt.

"Here." Gracie set a small box on the table and sat down beside him. She took his hand.

The soft scent of her lilac and honey perfume swarmed around him. He wanted to push aside the baseball cap, allow her hair to fall around her shoulders and kiss her.

She held his hand with a gentle touch. "I'm going to take the flannel off. It's going to sting. But we need to get the wound cleaned and then bandaged. You may need stitches." Her eyes searched his. "We can call Eric at the fire department and see if he is available to come over."

Adam gasped as Gracie pulled back the flannel. Blood dripped onto the table. "I'm sorry," he said.

"Don't apologize." Gracie tightened her lips. She opened a small package of wipes and a bottle of antiseptic.

The liquid stung as it hit his hand, and he flinched.

"Hold on." Gracie tightened her hand around his wrist. "It'll just take a minute."

With the skill and precision of a nurse, she wiped

away the blood and wrapped a clean bandage around his hand. She kept the pressure on his wrist. "I want to see if the blood will stop. If not, I'll call Eric."

Gracie looked up and their eyes met. His stomach churned, and not with the anxiety or because of his hurt wrist, but with something else. Something warmer and deeper.

He raised his left hand and removed a strand of hair dangling close to her left eye.

Gracie's breathing sharpened. The pressure on his wrist tightened.

She looked at him as his pulse raced. He could feel her breath, short and shallow as he leaned closer to her lips. Closer until they were inches from each other.

"Here you two are!"

Aunt Celia bustled into the kitchen with a large basket of fresh flowers. "I was just at the Farmers Market. What a wonderful Farmer's Market…" Her voice trailed off. "Oh! I'm interrupting."

"No, you're not." Gracie straightened. "Adam was hurt and I was just cleaning his wound."

She lifted her hand. It trembled slightly. Adam inhaled deep breaths. "I don't see any blood." He raised his hand. The bandage stayed snug and white.

"Blood?" Aunt Celia said. "I don't do very well with blood. I think I will just head to the living room and get a cup of tea." She dropped the basket of fresh flowers on the counter.

"The flowers are beautiful." Gracie stood and took a

bouquet of fresh pink and white tulips out of the basket. "I'll get a couple of vases and set these out in the living room and entryway."

"I'm going to head out." Adam stood. The room spun around him and then steadied. He was pretty sure it didn't have anything to do with the wound on his hand. "I'll grab the tools on the way out and stick them in the truck. I can come back in the morning and finish up."

"No," Gracie said, her voice firm. "Your hand needs to rest. I'll talk to Katie and Rylee and see if Bryan and Sawyer can come over and finish up. This is about all of us working together."

Adam nodded. Gracie was right. Even though he wanted to tackle the project on his own, they were all pitching in for the wedding.

He stared into Gracie's bright blue eyes. The memory of their almost kiss danced around the edges of his mind. He wanted to kiss her now. But did she want to kiss him? Or was it just a moment because she was swayed by the impact of their closeness and being hurt?

Her eyes warmed and a small smile crossed her lips. "If you want to stop by Sasha's and pick up some scones, I have a few guests who would enjoy them."

"I will do that," Adam said. "And a few for us." He winked at her.

A flush broke across Gracie's cheeks. The flush spread to her ears, and he warmed to her. It wasn't just him. She had been affected by the almost kiss, too.

Adam opened the back screen door, whistling a tune

he hadn't thought about since childhood. *Somewhere Over the Rainbow.* His steps were lighter as he turned around and softly shut the screen door, Gracie's small smile sending butterflies of joy into his chest. Joy he couldn't remember the last time he had felt.

Chapter 8

racie pushed open the back door of the inn. She picked up the rake, shovel, and weed trimmer and set them inside the gazebo. She brushed aside dirt, dead leaves, and pine needles and sat down inside the gazebo. Paint was peeling off on all the boards of the gazebo. It would need to be removed and sanded before they could paint a new coat. She hoped the weather would cooperate. Spring weather often meant bursts of rain and cloud cover with temperatures hovering in the high 50s. Not ideal for outdoor painting projects.

She ran her hands alongside the bench and replayed the almost kiss with Adam. It had been so unexpected, yet at the same time, it felt like the exact right thing to happen in the moment. But now what would happen? Could they go back to being just friends, or would it feel awkward and uncomfortable? Getting involved with Adam now was foolish. He was going to move to

Montana if the job offer came in or somewhere else far away from Cranberry Bay. He'd made that clear. The jobs he was looking for were not in Cranberry Bay. And she couldn't move. She had her inn which had just established itself, her supportive friends, and a community she had come to love.

She stood and walked to the other side of the gazebo, where what looked like a couple of branches lay across the bench. She picked it up and turned it over. Instead of it being two sticks, it was two sticks entwined together in the shape of a heart. Gracie turned the heart over but there weren't any markings or information about the heart.

"Gracie?" Maddie rode her bike into the backyard. She parked it next to the gazebo. She wore her hair pushed back in a rainbow-colored headband and her curls bounced on her shoulders. A long white t-shirt hung over her cut-off blue jean shorts. She wore a green all-weather jacket, and painted purple toenails peeked out from white sandals. Maddie dressed based on her mood for the day. Today, it seemed she felt like summer with a little bit of a practical mindset tossed in.

"Maddie." Gracie shook herself out of her thoughts. "It's Saturday. I lost track of the days with the wedding planning." Gracie was pretty sure it wasn't the wedding planning that was causing her mind to be a little forgetful.

"Who created the heart?" Maddie pointed to the heart stick in her hands.

"I don't know," Gracie said. "I found it lying on the gazebo bench."

"It looks like someone knew what they were doing with carving." Maddie turned the heart over in her hand. "Twigs don't just go together like this."

"No." Gracie shook her head. "They don't."

"Do we have a lot of rooms to clean?" Maddie replaced the heart on the gazebo bench.

"Not a full house today," Gracie said. "I believe it's just two rooms we are turning over tonight to new guests."

"I was wondering…" Maddie stopped, her face flushed.

Gracie waited.

"Would it be okay for me to leave a little early? The Wildlife Center is having an open house and I volunteered to set up a table to work with kids who want to learn more about Cormie. I know I'm supposed to work for you today…"

"It sounds like a wonderful opportunity!" Gracie said. "I know how much you enjoy helping out with the kids and educating them about Cormie the Cormorant is a great thing."

Cormie the Cormorant had been injured in the wild and came to the Wildlife Center. But the volunteers had fallen in love with him and realized that the bird enjoyed showing off in his tank for visitors. He'd become the Wildlife Center mascot, and everyone enjoyed sharing his habitat with small groups of visitors.

Maddie smiled. "I will get the rooms cleaned up and the laundry done."

"Why don't you let me handle the rooms today?"

Gracie said. "Aunt Celia can manage the front desk. How about you gather up the sheets and towels and run a couple loads of laundry?"

"Really?" Maddie reached out and hugged her. "You are the best!"

She embraced Gracie and hurried into the inn.

Gracie smiled. She had a passion for the environment, the same as her Uncle Adam. In all the college applications talk, there hadn't been much discussion about what Maddie planned to major in. Sawyer was pushing for business. He thought Maddie had a strong head for numbers and would work well with finance. Bryan thought she would be great in sales. But Gracie wasn't convinced of either option, and was pretty sure neither was Maddie.

Gracie stepped out of the gazebo carrying the twig heart and headed toward the screen door leading to the kitchen.

As she entered the kitchen, the phone rang and she moved to the small wooden desk she'd placed in a tiny alcove. She refused to cut her landline and maintained an old-fashioned telephone with a cord in the kitchen, and another one on the desk in the front entryway for reservations. She liked knowing that the inn calls were coming to a physical location and not her cell phone. The worst thing was going hiking and feeling chained to answering her calls.

Before she could answer the phone, Aunt Celia picked it up at the front desk. "New Leaf Inn. Can I help you?" Her voice was cheerful and carried throughout the front hallway.

Gracie shook her head and smiled. Aunt Celia hadn't seemed too enthusiastic for the invitation to the upcoming tea at the library, but she had jumped with all her enthusiasm into the inn's responsibilities. Gracie hadn't noticed any more disturbing phone calls, and the tiredness Gracie had worried about seemed to have vanished. She'd noticed her aunt snacking on more than one cookie as she sat at the front desk. Maybe Aunt Celia had just been stressed about too much on her plate and the slower pace of Cranberry Bay was helping her relax.

Gracie walked into the front hallway and placed the twig heart on the bench seat.

Maddie came down the stairs with a large pile of sheets and towels in her arms. She wrinkled her nose. "How long were the people in the Sunflower room?"

Gracie laughed. Maddie always had different things to say about the guests as she cleaned the rooms. Her insights were a good perspective and helped Gracie decide who to add to the do not allow to return list and which ones to place a star by their name and mark as favorite guests. Maddie dropped the pink and flowered paisley sheets on the ground. She rubbed her forearms. "Well, they must have hiked every trail around here in the rain. The floor is covered with dirt and grim, and the beds…" She shook her head.

"Thanks Maddie," Gracie said. "I'll give the room a hard scrub." Gracie was grateful to have Maddie's help on Saturdays and Sundays when the inn was the busiest.

But she did all the hard cleaning, which included scrubbing the clawfoot bathtubs in two of the rooms, and polishing the wood floors.

Aunt Celia stepped out from behind the desk. She carried a teacup in one hand and picked up the twig heart with the other. "What's this, Gracie? Did you make it?"

Gracie shook her head. "It was lying on one of the benches in the gazebo. I'm not sure if it was used as a decoration for an event in the gazebo or if someone made it and left it there."

"It would make a lovely decoration in the garden," Aunt Celia said. "We could also have some lanterns and twinkle lights along the gazebo, and maybe even a few tiki torches."

Gracie bit back her smile. "Those sound wonderful, although I'm not sure the tiki torches would fit the fire code." The last thing she needed was the fire chief citing her.

"Who is the fire chief?" Aunt Celia's eyes sparkled. "I am sure he can be persuaded." She winked at Maddie.

"Eric Adams is very happily married," Gracie said and shook her head. Small towns had a limited number of eligible bachelors. And with all the marriages and engagements of her friends over the last few years, the numbers have shrunk even more. When Adam moved away for his job that would be one less single man. Of course, she wasn't looking for anyone to fall in love with, especially Adam.

Maddie giggled. "Love is in the air." She did a small twirl. "Do you need help with anything else?"

"I think that's it." Gracie picked up the clipboard hanging on a small peg on the wall by the front desk. She hoped Aunt Celia and Maddie didn't notice the flush in her cheeks. Love was in the air, but did she want love with Adam? Did he want love with her?

The rooms all had check marks alongside their names. She made a small note by the Sunflower room with her name. She'd do the cleaning later today. There wasn't anyone booked in the room for two nights. But she liked to have all her rooms ready, just in case a guest stopped by without a reservation like her Aunt. It didn't happen often at this time of the year, but in the summer when the beach hotels were completely filled, she often got the overflow for a night or two. Unsuspecting visitors who had mistakenly believed they could drive the Oregon Coast and find last minute reservations in the popular beach towns in the height of summer.

"I'm going to Katie's for the sewing group. Would you like a ride to the Wildlife Center?"

Maddie flushed. "Lars is picking me up and taking me to the Wildlife Center. Is it okay if I leave my bike tucked behind the gazebo?"

"Of course." Gracie smiled.

Maddie had adjusted to her life in Cranberry Bay at the same time as Gracie. She and her mom, Lisa, the Shuster brothers' younger sister, had moved into the carriage house at Sawyer's. Maddie had been an angry young lady, who wore all black, thick black makeup, and long dark hair which covered her eyes.

But Cranberry Bay had softened her with their support, positive encouragement, and inclusion. Gradually Maddie had shed her protective shell and blossomed into a beautiful teenager, finishing the last semester of her senior year.

Gracie picked up her canvas bag containing her embroidery floss, a couple pieces of white canvas fabric, and a half-finished holiday piece. As the only one in the sewing circle who did not enjoy machine sewing, she loved working on her embroidery, sitting in a chair beside a wall of windows overlooking Katie and Sawyer's sprawling five-acre property.

"I should be home by four, although, it might be a little later. Sasha has some wedding ideas she wants us to work on."

Aunt Celia took a sip of her tea and leaned against the front desk. "I'm covering the desk. Go enjoy the wedding planning." She winked. "It might be your turn next."

Gracie flushed from her ears to her toes. She walked by the bench and picked up the heart. She might as well take it to the sewing circle. They could come up with ideas for what to do with it in the garden or maybe the wedding.

Ten minutes later, Gracie pulled her car into Katie's driveway. She drove down the gravel road and parked alongside the renovated barn. The doors stood open, and sunshine poured inside. Gracie slipped out of her car and headed into the barn.

At the large table in the center of the room, Rylee, Katie, Sasha, and Ivy sipped tea and pored over a handful of colorful dress design patterns. A catchy Ray Charles tune played from Katie's sound system.

"Gracie!" Katie waved her over. "There you are! We were getting worried."

Gracie set her canvas bag and the twig heart on the table.

"What is this?" Sasha picked up the twig heart. "Did you make this?"

"I found it in the gazebo," Gracie said. "I thought it would look nice hanging from the gazebo or maybe a pergola in the yard? It seems pretty sturdy. Or we could thread some white tulle through it and decorate it a bit more."

"I saw another one of these hearts the other day." Rylee frowned. "I'm not sure..." She paused. "The library! It was hanging from a tree in the library!"

"Maybe it's a new trend," Ivy said. "Leaving hearts around town. It's a little late for Valentine's Day but love is great anytime." She checked her phone and her face softened. "Izzy is sleeping. Josh just sent a picture."

"Mmmm...." Rylee said. "I think that's the tenth picture he's sent in the last ten minutes."

"He loves Izzy," Ivy said. "Just like I do. We don't want to miss a minute."

"I'm sorry. I didn't mean to sound so mean." Rylee's

cheeks flushed. "Bryan and I are not having much luck on the baby front. I'm really happy for you, Ivy."

Ivy touched Rylee's arm. "I'm sorry," she said. "I know how much you both want a baby."

"It will happen." Rylee squared her shoulders. "We're talking about adoption, too."

"Adoption would be wonderful. You and Bryan will make great parents." Katie carried a bolt of yellow fabric to the cutting table. "Maybe someone is leaving the hearts on purpose, like the yarn bombers."

"The yarn bombers?" Gracie asked.

"They bomb areas with yarn," Katie said with a smile. "They wrap yarn around power poles, trees, anything. It's very colorful."

"How about this one?" Sasha pushed a pattern to the center of the table. The tea length wedding dress had a halter tie with a heart neckline. A bow was place in on the front, right in the middle, while a stain tie hung down the back.

"That's perfect!" Katie said. "I have a bolt of ivory satin, and we can order more if needed from my distributor. It will be fun and flatter your figure well."

"What about bridesmaid dresses?" Rylee fingered the yellow fabric. "I'm not sure I look great in yellow."

"It's going to be a small private ceremony," Sasha said and bit her lower lip. "I'd love for all of you to be in the wedding, but if all of you are in the wedding, there will be no one in the audience!"

"But you need to have one of us as a Maid of

Honor," Rylee said. "I'm not volunteering myself." She shook her head. "I just don't look good in yellow."

"Izzy keeps me pretty busy," Ivy said. "I would love to just be in the audience if you don't mind?"

"I agree," Katie said. "You should have a Maid of Honor and Greg should have a Best Man. Sawyer and I are going to be so busy with the reception at the barn that I'm afraid we aren't a good option."

"Well." Sasha cleared her throat. "You know I love all of you dearly and I don't know what I would do without each one of you. But if I can only have one person, I'd like it to be Gracie."

Gracie inhaled. She hadn't expected Sasha to choose her as the Maid of Honor. Sasha had known the rest of the women for much longer. She and Ivy often spent time together driving into Portland for antique auctions or scouting out a new bakery.

"Me?" Gracie rested her hand on her chest.

"Yes," Sasha said, smiling at her. "You are calm and levelheaded, and I think I might need that on the day of my wedding. And," she smiled at the other women, "everyone else seems to have a reason for why they don't want to be the Maid of Honor."

"You'll need a dress." Katie thumbed through a large pattern book. "How about this one?"

Gracie walked to the table. The pink tea length off-the-shoulder dress flared above the knees. "Pink?" Gracie couldn't imagine wearing pink anything. Even in the plans for her own wedding, her bridesmaid dresses had all been pale yellow, the same color as the bolt of fabric Katie had placed on the table.

"How about a pale green?" Sasha leaned over Gracie's shoulder. "It will go well with your coloring."

Gracie nodded. Her heart raced. She had hoped to hide in the background of the wedding, attending to the details of the garden. But now she was going to be in the wedding. Standing in front, beside Sasha. Would she be able to get through the wedding without thinking about the one she almost had?

Sasha squeezed her hand. "I'm so happy you will be there with me."

Gracie swallowed the fear and anxiety coursing through her. She remembered the times Sasha and the other women in the sewing circle had been there for her. When she first moved to Cranberry Bay, they'd all reached out and helped her find the necessary resources she needed for the inn. They had supported her through the paperwork she needed to complete with the city to get the necessary permits and connected her with the people she needed to know to make sure the rooms were all in working condition. Including fixing toilets, repairing floorboards, and tightening seals around leaking windows. She never could have taken on the inn without the support of her friends in Cranberry Bay.

"I'm happy to be your Maid of Honor," Gracie said. A small flutter danced in her stomach. If Sawyer wasn't going to be Greg's Best Man, who would it be?

Chapter 9

"Thank you, Adam," Drew said, his voice clear and bright on the Zoom screen. "We really enjoyed getting to know you and will be in touch soon."

Adam exited the interview and leaned back in his chair. He took a deep breath. He thought the interview went well. He talked about his time at Wildlife Center as well his years working for the State Parks. The conversation had flowed easily with some laughter along the way.

Adam picked up his cell phone and texted Seth. *Interview went well.*

Seth's text immediately came across his screen. *Take it one day at a time. Breathe.*

Adam smiled. Sobriety wasn't easy, and he still had days when the craving would creep up on him and having Seth as his sponsor helped kept him grounded. It helped to check in with him about his day to day. Luckily, today wasn't a hard day.

If he got the job, he'd need to get himself established in the local AA as soon as he arrived, starting with meetings and getting a new sponsor. But he already had a connection. He'd spotted the small *Easy Does It* sign on Drew's desk during the interview. One thing he'd learned about being sober and in AA was the power of the fellowship stretched everywhere. Alcoholism had no limits or boundaries to who it affected.

Going to pick up Gracie and head to the nursery in Pelican Shores. Adam texted.

Sounds great. Seth texted back. *Suzanne and I are headed out with the kayaks today.*

Adam pocketed his phone and headed out the door. He got into his truck and started the engine. He hadn't seen Gracie since their almost kiss a few days ago. He wanted to talk to her about the interview, but nerves fluttered inside him. Would their friendship change with that one almost kiss?

He drove down the gravel road and out of the state park. One part of sobriety was he had to feel all his feelings. Before, he'd always drowned them with alcohol. Any feeling he didn't want to feel, which included pretty much all of them, he simply drank them away.

Gracie never told him the details of her almost marriage, but he knew there had been pain involved, both physical and mental. He'd seen the tell-tale signs of old bruises and scars when she first arrived in Cranberry Bay. Over time, most of them had faded and she came out of her shell as she'd been embraced by the warmth and kindness of the small town. But he still saw the edge, the flinches when no one else was watching.

He'd listened to stories in AA and he knew physical and emotional abuse took a long time to heal. The last thing he wanted to do was ruin their friendship. And both had sworn off love. But the emotions played around the edges of his heart. He wouldn't be able to pretend he didn't have feelings for her. He worked through an honesty program in AA and part of his honesty was admitting he had feelings, both good and bad. And these were good feelings. Very good.

Adam pulled up alongside the inn as Gracie deadheaded a couple flowers in the front entry pot. She wore dark jeans, a light blue windbreaker, and her hair was pulled back in a ponytail. A large bag hung over her shoulder. She waved and walked toward the truck. Adam leaned over, opening the door and Gracie slipped in.

Her fresh clean scent filled the truck cabin, and he took in a deep breath. He cleared his throat and tried to tell her hello, but his tongue stuck to the roof of his mouth. He felt like he was fourteen again on his first date.

"I worked on the map of the backyard." Gracie reached into her bag. "But I didn't have a chance to make any notes about what types of plants we need."

"I've got a list," Adam said. The words returned to him. He always did well with a plan, and they were working on a project. "It's on the clipboard in the back seat." There wasn't enough room in the backseat of his truck to have passengers, but the small space gave him some room to put things like water bottles and clipboards. Adam kept a clipboard for each part of his life. He had one for the Wildlife Center, one for jobs to do at the park, one with notes for his personal errands, and now one for Gracie's backyard project.

Gracie turned around and reached toward the back. "Which one?"

"It should be on top," Adam said. "Yellow tablet attached."

"Got it."

Adam kept his eyes on the road, trying to distract himself from her and a new wave of her soft scent as she shifted closer to him to reach into the back. She settled back in her seat with the clipboard in hand.

A light rain fell on the windshield as Gracie read the list of plants. "Pink, yellow, and white rhododendron. Blue hydrangea. Lavender." She tapped the clipboard. "What about some flowers? We should get some large pots like we have in front. Maybe some hanging baskets inside the gazebo."

"Good idea." Adam tapped the steering wheel, a picture forming in his mind of the yard in bloom. "I chose plants that would be blooming during the wedding and that grow well in our coastal soil. Too many people choose plants they like but don't pay attention to the coastal environment." He shook his head. He had worked hard to plant only native plants on the park trails, clearing away the invasive plants like ivy and blackberry which threatened to overtake trees and pathways. People loved the blackberry vines and the berries they produced, but the blackberries easily grew into an obnoxious weed if they weren't kept trimmed.

"These will cover the yard well," Gracie said. "While at the same time leaving room for the walkway."

"We can pick up some pavers, too." Adam stopped at a light. The rain intensified, and he moved the wipers to a faster speed. "The Sea Shore Cove superstore hardware is just a couple blocks away." He liked to be prepared, and he'd called ahead yesterday to make sure the pavers were in stock.

The light turned green and he pulled into a side lane to pass a slow RV. "I had my interview for the Montana job, and it seemed to go—" Adam stopped as his phone rang, the Wildlife Center name flashing across his hands-free screen.

"Hey, Angie," Adam said after he clicked the button on his steering wheel.

"I've got an update on the puffin," Angie said.

"You're on speaker," he said. "I've got Gracie in the car with me." He always made sure people on the phone knew when he had someone in the car with him. Cranberry Bay was a small town, and although Sea Shore Cove and Pelican Shores were bigger, town gossip could be fierce. One person knew someone else who knew someone else. It was best to be upfront.

Angie had teased him about his friendship with Gracie, hinting there could be something more. And the last thing he wanted was for her teasing words to upset Gracie.

"The puffin is doing well," Angie said. "Bill was here

to take care of the wing. It's recovering well and has been eating and drinking like normal."

Adam exhaled. "That's great news."

Beside him, Gracie visibly relaxed. Both knew how important it was for the puffin to recover for the Wildlife Center's reputation.

"How about the Wildlife Director search?" Adam said. He hoped they could hire the new director before he took a job somewhere else. He felt protective of the Wildlife Center and its bird patients.

Angie sighed. "That's not going so well. It's hard to fill a part-time position. Everyone needs full time."

Adam nodded. It was why he hadn't applied for the Wildlife Center position himself. He needed health care benefits and a full-time salary which was hard to find in environment jobs.

"How was your interview?"

"It went well," Adam said. "I should hear back in a couple days." He looked at Gracie out of the corner of his eye. She sat straight as a board and stared ahead. Her face gave nothing away about how she felt.

"Well, keep me posted," Angie said. "I gotta go. It's feeding time. Talk to you later."

Adam clicked the phone to off and pulled into the parking lot of the plant nursery.

"I'm glad the interview went well." Gracie turned to him, her face unreadable.

Conflicting emotions coursed through Adam. He wanted this job. It was perfect for him, and although he would miss his friends and family in Cranberry Bay, he knew he could make a difference with this job. But at the same time, something else tugged at him. Something he hadn't expected to feel. A softening toward Gracie and a feeling he didn't dare name.

Instead of responding to Gracie, he mumbled. "Let's go see about those plants."

A few hours later, Adam lifted another heaping shovel of dirt and dropped it on the mound beside him. "Looks like we've got enough space for the first plant."

Gracie sprinkled organic fertilizer into the hole and stepped back. Adam lifted the rhododendron out of the large black pot. The roots wound around the pot and out the holes on the bottom. He pulled the plant upward, careful not to break any of the branches or unopened buds. Gracie admired Adam's gentle yet firm touch. Plants that sat for too long often became root-bound. As long as the roots were not broken too badly when the plant was removed from the plant, it could reestablish itself in the soil.

Adam placed the plant in the hole. Gracie shoveled dirt around the plant, careful to only pull dirt from the pile that wasn't covered with small weeds and grasses. Weeds and grasses easily took hold and she didn't want to use weed killers on the cleared backyard. As long as she kept up with the yard, the weeds shouldn't grow out of control again. When the new plant was covered, she knelt and patted the ground with her hand shovel and then her hands, smoothing the soil into place.

Gracie brushed her hands on her jeans. "I think that's it for this one."

"Only a few more to go." Adam waved his hand toward the row of plants lined alongside the gazebo.

Gracie felt happier than she had in a long time. She and Adam were working together to make a beautiful space for Sasha and Greg's wedding. All of her worries about Sasha's wedding preparations triggering her own painful memories had fallen away. She only felt happiness for her friend. And it was so easy to work with Adam. Although she'd walked with him often on the trails and beaches and spent time with him working on Cranberry Bay festivals and events, it had never been the two of them working together on a specific project like her backyard.

She pushed a strand of hair out of her face. She had dreaded working together with her ex- fiancé, Mike. Everything seemed to end in a disagreement of some sort and him getting drunk. Most of the time she had remained silent, learning not to voice her opinions for fear of his anger. She'd told herself he would settle down when they got married but deep down, she'd known it wouldn't happen.

That was the problem with abusive relationships. There was a part of her that always hoped things would be better the next day. It was the hope that kept her from leaving, the hope in the illusion of who he could be, not who he was. When she first arrived in Cranberry Bay, she had attended a handful of therapy sessions with a woman the local domestic violence shelter had recommended. She'd learned why it had been so hard for her to leave Mike and tried to forgive herself for staying so long.

A drop of rain fell on Adam's head and he adjusted his wide-brimmed canvas hat she'd often seen him wearing on hikes and cleaning trails. "If there is one thing we can count on in Oregon spring is rain."

"Always," Gracie said and laughed. She wasn't wearing a hat and rain drops fell into her hair.

Adam grinned. "Let's get the next one in the ground. At least we won't have to water them."

Gracie worked beside Adam, helping him to carry the plant to the next space they'd mapped out. They had pinned the map on one of the gazebo poles. She'd slipped the map into a plastic protective covering, ensuring that the rain wouldn't ruin their work.

Her body relaxed. It was easy to work with Adam. He was predictable and didn't have moods that fluctuated wildly. He didn't yell at her or tell her she had done something wrong and as they worked, and she found herself relaxing and slipping into the easy companionship she'd enjoyed with him on the trails. She pushed the almost kiss from her mind. It was easier to think of Adam as a friend, nothing more.

After two more rhododendrons were planted, the light rain turned into a steady drizzle. Gracie's hair plastered to her head and even though she zipped her jacket around her, the chill crept in. A burst of rain poured from the sky, drenching her.

"Come on." Adam reached for her shovel, their hands touching. "Let's get inside the gazebo."

Gracie ducked under the cover and Adam followed. He placed the shovel alongside one of the bench seats framing the gazebo. A row of marigolds, geraniums, small white flowers, and petunias sat on the seat bench. Large colorful pots piled alongside the back of the gazebo. The flowers would frame the spot where Sasha and Greg would say their vows. Rain pattered on the top of the gazebo which was still covered with ivy and black-berry vines. It would take a few more gardening days to finish cleaning up the area. Gracie shivered.

"Cold?" Adam slipped off his jacket. "Take my jacket."

"Thank you." She'd worn her hiking jacket and although it was warm, it wasn't like the fleece-lined all-weather coat Adam wore. Being outside in all elements of weather, he had better protection than she did.

Adam held out the jacket. Gracie turned and slipped her arms inside. The jacket hung around her small frame. Adam stepped in front of her and zipped it half-way up.

"Better?" His dark eyes gazed into hers and her stomach quivered.

"Yes," she said, her voice soft.

Adam didn't step away. Her pulse raced but she didn't move away from him either.

The small set of white lights she'd placed around the gazebo turned on and glowed in the darkening day.

He removed a wet strand of hair from her check. But instead of removing his hand, he caressed her face, tracing the outline of her forehead down to her chin. His thumb brushed her cheek, sending arcs of warmth through her.

"Gracie," Adam said, his voice soft and husky. "I really want to…"

She didn't let him finish, tilting her head upward and met his lips.

Gracie drank in the earthy, woodsy scent of Adam's mouth. Opening to him, her hands moved over his solid chest and upward along the back of his neck She caressed his neck. He groaned softly and pressed against her. His body was warm and solid. The chill had gone from her and a new sensation was taking hold.

A dog barked and in a burst of energy, Max, bounded into the gazebo and pressed against Gracie and Adam.

"Max!" Gracie broke away from Adam's lips and embrace. Flustered, she reached down and grabbed her dog. "Who let you out?" The gate wasn't closed. They'd left it open as they brought in the plants. "The gate is still open!"

"Sorry!" Aunt Celia called from the open kitchen door. "I didn't realize the gate was open! The rain is really coming down!"

Gracie held onto Max's collar and tried to shake the lingering effects of Adam's kiss away.

"I've got to go get him inside," she said. "His leash is by the front door, and he can't be out here right now. All the mud on his paws! It will make a mess in the inn." Gracie's guests loved Max. She made sure to put pictures of him on the website and warn guests there was a dog on the premises so there were no surprises or guests who were allergic. But guests weren't so forgiving of muddy paw prints on couches or chairs.

"I'll get him." Adam reached down and placed his hands on Gracie's. His large hand closed over hers, warm and solid.

Max wiggled underneath her hand. "Hold still," Gracie said, her voice sharp and firm. She reached into her pocket and pulled out two treats. She held them in front of Max's nose. He stopped squirming and took both treats.

Adam reached under his flannel shirt to his jeans and pulled off his belt. He tied it around Max's collar. "There we go," he said. "Let's get him into the house." He held out his hand and because it seemed the most natural thing in the world, Gracie slipped hers into his warm one. He squeezed her fingers, his thumb caressing her palm, sending shivers through her which had nothing to do with the weather.

"Do you have a towel?" Adam opened the kitchen door. Max pulled ahead on his belt leash. The smell of chocolate chip cookies filled the kitchen. A tray of warm chocolate chip cookies sat on a plate with two glasses of iced tea beside them.

"Over here." Gracie reached around the door and grabbed a green towel from a hook.

Adam took the towel, leaned down and rubbed Max until the dog's fur was only slightly damp and the mud was gone from his paws. He couldn't remember the last time he felt this happy. He'd always loved being around Gracie, the way she looked at the world with curiosity. Although she was a little reserved, she hadn't allowed the events in her life to harden her. But after that kiss, he felt something else. Something he hadn't dreamed or hoped could happen again after the kayak accident.

He had resolved himself to his life as it was now, not as he had once dreamed of sharing it with someone he loved. He didn't believe he could be a good husband and father and that it was best not to get romantically involved with anyone. But now, he felt that feeling again of wanting romantic companionship.

He enjoyed being with Gracie and hoped she felt the same way, too. She hadn't resisted when he'd held out his hand. It seemed so natural, so right. But now it was hard to read her as she bustled around the kitchen, straightening the flour and sugar canisters which were already straight and wiping down the spotless counter. Was she freaking out about the kiss?

A bright burst of sunlight shone through the window, across the black and white tiled floor. "Looks like the sun is out. We can finish up the plants today." He pulled out his cell phone. He needed to text Seth and let him know he didn't need a ride to the AA meeting.

Planting flowers with Gracie, he texted. *Going to miss the AA meeting.*

Relationships are *important.* Seth texted back. *Glad to hear you are spending time with Gracie. But remember to keep up with your meetings. It's easy to spiral into a relapse.*

Adam grimaced. He knew attendance at his AA meetings was important and he never missed one, especially the noon meeting he attended with Seth. Sobriety should always come first. He didn't have a life without sobriety first. But it was also important that he helped with the yard.

And he had to admit he didn't want to leave Gracie yet. He took a long, deep breath. Gracie's kiss was the best kiss he ever had. He couldn't remember ever kissing anyone else the way he had just kissed Gracie. She had a softness and yet a strength to her. The way she smelled like clean sheets freshly removed from a clothesline on a spring day with a hint of lavender. But even more, he loved how he felt when he was around her. As if nothing in the world would ever disturb him again.

I'll go to a meeting tonight. Adam texted. He'd been sober for four years but it was still important to go to meetings on a regular basis. He'd heard the stories of how it started with a missed meeting or two, then the texts and calls to a sponsor becoming sporadic. And then it was just a matter of time before that slip happened. Seth was a good sponsor and worked hard to help Adam keep his sobriety. But missing one meeting wasn't going to hurt anything, especially if he was going to attend a meeting tonight.

His phone buzzed and his mom's name flashed across the screen. "Mom?" He answered and stepped out of the kitchen. "Everything okay?"

"I'm sorry to bother you," Rebecca Shuster said. "But I have a doctor's appointment in Pelican Shores. It's an eye appointment and you know I don't like to drive after those. Bryan was supposed to take me but…"

"He got a showing," Adam said. Bryan's uncertain schedule due to his real estate showings was legendary. "What about Sawyer?"

"I don't want to bother him," Rebecca said. "You know how busy he is."

Adam bit back the words. His brothers had demanding careers that were unpredictable with scheduling. He knew that they supported their mom financially and she never lacked for anything. He couldn't support his mom with money. His salary just wasn't that big. But hopefully if he got the new job, he would be able to do a better job giving her money for special things, especially because he wouldn't be able to see her as much.

"It's okay, Mom," he said. "I'll take you. Be there in ten minutes." He would have to wait for the rest of the plants. Mom liked to go to dinner and spend a little time browsing the shops in Pelican Shores, and by the time he got back it would be dark. He wouldn't be able to make the AA meeting either. But he didn't need to tell Seth about his second missed meeting. He wasn't newly sober when he had to go to a meeting every day for the first ninety days. He was allowed to skip a meeting here and there.

Adam stepped back into the kitchen. His stomach felt heavy. He hated to disappoint anyone, especially Gracie. The yard was a project he'd promised to work on with her. It took two of them to do the planting and they still had about half a dozen plants left to go.

Tomorrow, he was supposed to work on one of the trails with a crew of volunteers while the weekend weather was warm and sunny. He wouldn't be able to get away from monitoring the entrance and making sure no one slipped in without a park pass or paying the day fee. He wanted to catch the free loading surfer guy before he left for another job. Adam wouldn't let him get away with not paying his fair share.

"Everything okay?" Gracie placed her rag on the

counter. A tiny flush formed on her cheeks, but it was the only indication for how she felt about their kiss.

"I need to take Mom to an appointment in Pelican Shores," he said. "I want to get the plants in the ground, but I won't be able to get back for a few days."

"I understand," Gracie said, her voice soft.

"It's supposed to be nice this weekend," Adam said, the words falling out of his mouth before he could stop them. He didn't want to wait to see Gracie again. He wanted to see her for more than just planting the bushes. He wanted her to know that she meant more to him than just a friend and their kiss wasn't just an accident. "Why don't we take a hike? The tide is supposed to be low, and we could do an early morning hike."

Max barked and jumped around.

"I think Max agrees with that idea," Gracie said, and smiled.

A smile broke across Adam's face. It wasn't just Max who liked the idea of a weekend hike. "I'll meet you at seven AM on Saturday at the parking lot to the beach trail," Adam said. A feeling of jubilation and euphoria rose in his chest. If Gracie had minded the kiss, she wouldn't have agreed to an early morning hike. She would have found some excuse, something with the inn, to say no. Was this a positive sign that Gracie felt the same about him as he was feeling about her? He hoped so.

Chapter 12

On Saturday morning, Gracie opened the car door and unhooked Max's leash from the back. He walked to the edge of the seat and jumped to the ground. She held onto his leash with one hand and grabbed her backpack, making sure her water bottle was secured to a loop on the side. She always made sure to carry Max's small, foldable bowl, water, a small bag of treats for Max, and a couple granola bars and trail mix for herself.

Max tugged on the leash. "I'm coming," Gracie said, and laughed. She loved Max. She hadn't planned on getting a dog. One day, Rylee had taken her dog, Raisin, to the vet for his shots. The vet who donated his time at the animal shelter told her about a Westie who wasn't adjusting to shelter life. They needed someone to foster the dog. Did Rylee know anyone who would adopt him? Rylee immediately called Gracie, and she agreed. As soon as Gracie saw Max, she fell in love with the dog and put in an application to adopt him.

Max loved the wide open beaches of the North Coast which were part of the state parks system. Dogs could run without being on leashes if they were under voice control. She'd taught him to come when called with his ball and treats. Sometimes they joined other local dogs and their owners for long low tide walks. Everyone made sure their dogs did not chase the seagulls or other sea birds. Max had gotten so used to not bothering the sea birds, Gracie never worried about calling for a bird rescue while walking Max.

"Max!" Adam leaned down and rubbed the dog's fur. He looked up and gave her a boyish grin. His truck was one of a handful of cars in the parking lot. In a few hours, the parking lot would be filled. But this early in the morning, only the bird watchers and a handful of people who wanted to explore the tide pools were there. The beach wasn't one of the popular ones in Seashore Cove. It was tucked out of the way and mostly drew locals and visitors who knew how to find hidden gems when they traveled.

Gracie's heart danced a quick beat as her eyes met Adam's. He wore a navy-blue windbreaker over a light blue sweatshirt. His eyes sparkled. She'd never noticed how much sparkle he had in his eyes before. Her pulse raced a little faster. She took a few deep breaths. She'd walked with Adam many times on this trail down to the beach. It was their favorite hike, and they enjoyed exploring the tide pools and watching the birds, especially the oyster catchers who made nests in the lower area of the rocks and were usually chased off by predators or humans.

There was no reason to be anxious. Adam wasn't like her ex. He never showed up drunk. Grateful to not have to worry about him drinking, she'd simply told him she didn't like alcohol. He'd introduced her to a local Portland brand of teas, and she made sure to always have them on hand at the inn.

Adam reached into his jacket pocket and gave Max a treat.

Gracie's insides warmed. Adam never carried dog treats. He didn't own a dog. The fact that he did meant he bought them from Paige at the local pet shop.

"Ready?" He pointed to the trail leading down to the beach.

Gracie slipped her backpack across both shoulders and followed behind Adam on the single person trail. Adam wanted to widen the popular trail but hadn't gotten approval from the parks as a necessary project. Now that his job had been terminated, Gracie doubted the trail would become a project at all.

The news about the budget cuts with the parks systems across the country was grim as thousands of people were laid off. Adam was lucky he got an interview with a city that purchased a building for an environmental center when so many were being laid off and unable to find replacement jobs in their love of the environment and stewardship. Her heart tugged at her. She didn't want him to leave, especially not after their kiss, but she also wanted him to have work that gave him purpose, even if that purpose didn't include her.

As they walked down the trail, Adam stopped and picked up small twigs, a couple pieces of trash, and a dog poop bag that had been left by the side of the trail. He unzipped his backpack and put the trash and poop bag into an outside pocket. Gracie had never known Adam not to take care of the trails. Even though his job had ended, he still protected the park he loved so much. She couldn't imagine the tree lighting without Adam working on the lights with Josh and Bryan. Or the Soups for Santa without Adam helping to load up the fire truck with canned goods as it stopped in all the neighborhoods.

"Gracie?" Adam said. "Is everything okay?"

"Sorry." Gracie shook herself out of her thoughts. Adam stopped walking and faced her. She needed to stay in the moment. Adam was still here. He hadn't left yet. She was ruining a good day by worrying about him leaving when it hadn't happened yet. It was a pattern she'd picked up with her ex-fiancé. She had to worry about him. She never knew what each day would bring and she had to be prepared. Adam wasn't like that. He was dependable and consistent. She didn't need to worry about a tomorrow that hadn't arrived yet.

"I was asking you about the pots for the gazebo. Do you think we will need a few more? There is a sale this week. I could pick some up."

"We might need one or two," Gracie said. "It's a big space and…" She flushed as the memory of their kiss in the gazebo flooded her mind.

For a minute, neither one of them said a word as the sounds of the forest stretched out around them. Birds chirped and called from their branches. The morning sunlight shone through the trees, casting arcs of light as it reflected off the morning dew in the fir tree branches. She'd always loved the morning hours, but she especially loved it since moving to Cranberry Bay and going on morning hikes. She learned to appreciate the stillness and quietness of the trails in all weather.

Max barked at something moving in the woods. He pulled on the leash and headed toward the sound.

"Easy, boy," Adam said. "Don't want to get yourself caught by a coyote."

Gracie gave the leash a hard tug. The coyotes weren't the only animals in the woods surrounding the trail. The biggest threat was the large herd of Roosevelt elk, especially during the rutting season when they became aggressive. Tourists often got too close to the elk when they were in the neighborhood parks. Every season, at least one dog had a near miss as they charged the elk.

The trail widened and Gracie walked beside Adam as Max bounded ahead, stretching the flexi leash to its full length. Paige had recommended multiple leashes for Max in their dog training class. She used a leather leash that could be adjusted in length when they walked around town or crowded trails, and the flexi leash when walking on trails that were not so crowded. Max loved to explore the woods, and with the flexi leash, she could allow him to sniff the plants and trees alongside the trails.

Ahead of them, a family of four stopped and a woman who looked to be in her thirties opened a backpack and pulled out three water bottles. She handed one to a boy and a girl and then took a large swallow out of one herself. A man who looked to be about the same age as the woman consulted a trail map.

Max stopped and sniffed at what looked like a bunch of twigs. He picked up what looked like a bundle with his mouth.

"Max!" Gracie said, her voice sharp. "Give that back!"

Gracie shortened the leash, leaned down, and picked up the bundle of twigs. "It's another heart." She turned it over in her hands. The heart had been constructed the same way as the one she'd found in the gazebo. "Rylee found one at the library, and I found one in the gazebo."

Gracie looked over at Adam, whose ears were red. "You don't know who is leaving these, do you?" she asked, smiling. It would be like Adam to leave the hearts. She didn't know why she didn't think of him before.

Adam, Tyler, Sawyer's daughter, Lauren, had left painted rocks with positive sayings all over town last summer. The three of them had tried to keep it a secret, but when Lauren showed up with paint on her hands for one of the Sunday brunches and Adam sheepishly handed Katie a tray with paint globs on it, the secret had been exposed. Afterward, Katie suggested they set up a designated table in the barn where they could make all the mess they needed and not use any of her kitchen trays.

"Maybe." Adam shrugged as the little girl ahead of them on the trail exploded into tears.

"I didn't want to go on this hike! I wanted to stay home!"

Adam stepped forward and touched the mother on the arm. "May I?"

The mother nodded and Adam knelt down beside the child. "The woods can sometimes be scary."

The girl stared at him as tears continued to roll down her face.

"But," Adam said, "there are all kinds of things to learn in the woods. Listen." He put his finger up to his ears.

The child cocked her head.

"Do you hear the birds?" Adam asked. "They're calling to each other. They speak a language just like us.

"And there are all kinds of great things to find," Adam said, his voice soft and patient.

Gracie's heart expanded as she watched Adam. He had such a good way with calming the child and showing her the natural beauty of the woods. Gracie stepped forward. She held out the twig heart in her hands. "Would you like this?"

The girl looked up at her wide-eyed.

"It will remind you of what you can find in the woods," Gracie said.

The girl nodded and took the heart.

"There's an interpretative center back on the left side of the parking lot," Adam said to the rest of the family. "There are lots of things to learn about the sea birds, tide pools, and woods."

"Thank you." The mother turned to Gracie. "And thank you."

Gracie smiled at Adam. She loved the gentleness and kindness he showed to everyone, including herself. She walked in front of Adam and took quick steps with Max trotting ahead of her. In minutes, Gracie reached the sandy shore, and the wide, empty beach stretched all around her. She took a deep breath. This was her favorite part of the trail. The moment she came out of the woods and stepped onto the beach, which seemed endless with possibilities.

She leaned down and unclipped Max's leash. He gave a little trot dance and ran off, sniffing the driftwood.

"I brought some breakfast." Adam unzipped his backpack. He pulled out two blueberry scones. "Sasha let me in a little early."

Gracie smiled. She knew how much Sasha guarded her eight AM open time. Even though she arrived at six AM to make the scones and muffins, she refused to let anyone in early and a small line always formed outside her bakery.

"How did you accomplish that?" Gracie took one of the scones. She bit into it and the soft moisture of the blueberry exploded in her mouth.

"Truth?" Adam said. "Greg was just arriving and she let him in. I traded Greg for a favor."

"What favor?" Gracie raised an eyebrow. A favor to Greg could be anything from helping out at the marina with the holiday ships parade to giving him a second opinion on one of his classic cars he liked to drive.

"He needed a Best Man."

Gracie swallowed. "A Best Man?" A Best Man favor was a lot to trade for scones.

Adam shrugged. "Greg wasn't really close to anyone in Seattle. He asked Sawyer but he said it would be too much for him to do with trying to host the reception at his place."

"Mmm…" Gracie took another bite of the scone. She chewed and swallowed. Her heartbeat picked up. They both were going to be in the wedding. Was it a coincidence, or were their well-meaning friends trying to help love along?

"I agreed," Adam said, his eyes gazing into hers. "It's a small wedding and everyone is family or friends."

A large eagle swooped above them as it moved from the tall evergreens out to the ocean. "I agreed to be the Maid of Honor," Gracie said. She didn't move her gaze from Adam. But her hands felt sweaty, and her pulse increased against her throat.

Adam stepped closer to her. "I know this is a big deal for you. Hosting the ceremony at the inn and now being the Maid of Honor."

Gracie swallowed. She'd told everyone that her marriage fell through in the days leading up to the wedding. But she'd never told anyone why. But something inside of her pushed at her. She wanted to tell Adam. She wanted him to know what had happened. He wouldn't judge her, and she trusted him to keep her secret. A secret wrapped in shame. Shame that she hadn't left her fiancé when the abuse first started. Shame that she'd stayed, hoping both the drinking and the abuse would get better. And then he'd left her for someone else. A little voice inside her head that was always telling her she hadn't been enough, she hadn't been *good* enough.

"I've told everyone that I didn't get married at the last minute, but I've never told anyone in Cranberry Bay why." She took a deep breath. The words bubbled inside her mouth.

Adam touched her hand. "I'm here for you."

Gracie took a deep breath. She trusted Adam. She knew he wouldn't tell everyone about her past or judge her.

"My fiancé was abusive," Gracie said. "He drank too much and when he was drunk, he physically abused me. I didn't want to leave him because I kept thinking it would change; things would get better. If I could just do something better, be a different person. But," her voice cracked. "He left me for someone else.

"I'm sorry." Adam held out his arms and Gracie stepped into them. His embrace was warm and comforting. "Nothing you could have done would change him. You don't deserve to be hit. Ever." His voice hardened.

"I know that intellectually," Gracie said. Her voice was soft now. "But it's hard to believe inside sometimes."

"There's somewhere I want to show you," Adam said, his voice quiet and soft. He held her close. "It's a special place that I like to keep to myself. But I'd like to share it with you."

Gracie pulled herself out of the warm embrace of his arms and looked up at him. His blue eyes gazed at her, soft and protective. She slipped her hand into his. "I'd like to see it."

Chapter 13

Adam touched the top of Gracie's hand, caressing it lightly. The soft spring air blew around her face pushing strands of hair into her eyes. He let go of her hand, reaching up to remove the strand of hair.

"Let's go this way." Adam cleared his throat. His voice sounded gruff and unnatural. But his emotions raced inside him like a waterfall in spring, cascading over the rocks. He felt closer to Gracie. He warmed knowing that she trusted him and opened up about her past. He wanted to do the same for her.

The sandy shore stretched out for miles in the low tide. Clusters of tide pools formed around the smaller sea stacks that were uncovered in the tide. A few people walked among them, but for the most part, the beach was still empty in the early morning. Gracie slipped off her shoes and held them between her fingers.

Max ran back and forth between Gracie and the

ocean water lapped at the sand. Each time he raced to Gracie's side, she slipped her hand into her pocket and pulled out a treat. Adam had stopped by the pet store yesterday and picked up the same brand of treats he'd seen Gracie giving to Max. After the third time Max ran to Gracie, he called for the dog, and when Max reached him, Adam reached into his pocket and gave a treat to Max.

Gracie laughed. "Now he has two people trained!"

Adam shrugged and smiled. He loved dogs, and the Oregon Coast was a dog's heaven with its wide sandy beaches. He'd always wanted his own dog, but his job kept him busy for hours on end, and he knew it wasn't fair to a dog to make it stay in his trailer all day.

Adam stopped when they reached an outcropping of large rocks. Because of the low tide, there was a way into the cave. "Come on," Adam said. "The tide is low enough and we have enough time before it goes out to go in and come back out."

"Are you sure?" Gracie studied the ocean. "I didn't check the tide timetable this morning. I knew it was low tide, and usually it doesn't matter when the tide comes in when getting back to the trail."

"I checked the timetable." Adam reached into his bag for the small tide book. There were multiple apps that showed the tide times, but none of them ever seemed to be right. The small booklet published by the Pelican Shores Aquarium was always correct to the minute. Most of the parks and seashore educators relied on it. He flipped the page to the table with today's date and showed Gracie the time. The tide was still going out for another twenty minutes. They had a good forty-five minutes before the tide would lap at the entrance to the cave.

He was used to Gracie questioning everything. It was something he'd noticed about her from their first walk. She liked to be one hundred percent sure about everything, checking and double-checking everything. Now, he understood why she asked questions and couldn't take things at face value.

Adam slipped the booklet back into his backpack and led the way. He walked inside the cave. Half-burnt candles sat on the rock shelves above them. Local teenagers often waded through the waters to reach the cave, so it wasn't a surprise to find empty bottles or candles strewn around. The high tide took the bottles out when they were left on the sandy ground, but the candles were kept out of the water on the higher rock shelves.

Adam reached into his pack and pulled out a set of matches. Even with the sunlight pouring in the opening, the cave still wasn't very bright. He struck the match on the cave wall and lit a candle. The flame flickered and a small notebook tucked into the back wall of the cave caught his eye. He reached for a small notebook. He'd been in the cave multiple times and never noticed the book. Someone must have left it or removed it and not tucked it back into its former hiding place. Carefully, Adam pulled the book out. The notebook had been wrapped in a plastic bag, the same kind he used to store his vegetables in the refrigerator for snacking.

Gracie perched on a rock ledge that worked as a bench seat, and he sat down beside her.

Their legs touched as he slipped the book out of the plastic. The pages were thick with handwritten notes, small pieces of artwork, and memorable stuck inside each page.

A folded note fell out onto the sand, and he picked it up and read it aloud.

Dear Caitlin,

I am leaving tomorrow for Afghanistan. I want you to know how much I love you. If something should happen, please come to this cave and get our book.

Love Robert

Gracie leaned over his shoulder and pressed up against him. "The book is still here. He surely must have made it home by now?"

"I hope so." Adam flipped the pages, careful not to let any of the notes, artwork, or ticket stubs fall out. "It looks like a record of their relationship."

Gracie touched a small piece of artwork. A whale with bubbles around it filled the small sheet of paper, which had been folded multiple times. She flipped it over. On the back, a note had been written in neat, cursive script. *Joyful love. Always, Caitlin*

Adam's chest warmed. Joyful love. That's what he felt when he was with Gracie. Joyful.

Gracie shivered.

"Cold?" Adam turned and slipped off his flannel jacket. He wore multiple layers of clothing. He'd learned it was easier to take off clothing than to not have enough on. He dropped his jacket around Gracie's shoulders.

"Thank you," Gracie said. "I always forget how cold it can be on these coastal walks. In St. Louis, we didn't have these cold springs like the Oregon Coast."

Adam chuckled. "I don't think anyone has the cold springs like the Oregon Coast." He smiled at her. "But everyone loves the warm September days." His heart contracted. This year, he wouldn't be here for the warm September days. Even if he didn't get the Montana job, he still needed a job and there weren't any on the Oregon Coast. In September, he would be somewhere else, without Gracie. His joy bubble popped.

"Adam?" Gracie touched his lower arm. "Are you okay?"

Adam shook himself out of the future. Future tripping, the AA guys called it. You had to take it one day at a time. He brought Gracie to the cave because he wanted to tell her about his past. He wanted her to know that he respected and honored *her* past, and that his wasn't a secret, either. They were friends. Friends who had kissed, but friends first and foremost. And friends told each other about their lives.

"I want to tell you something. Something that happened to me."

Adam swallowed. He'd never told the story of what happened in the kayak accident. Not even to Seth. But he wanted to tell Gracie. He wanted her to know everything about him. He wanted her to know she could trust him, and he didn't keep secrets.

"I want to tell you something. Something about my past. You shared yours with me and I want you to know me, too." He took a deep breath. "Amy, my long-time girlfriend, wanted me to give her niece a kayaking lesson. It was late in the afternoon, and I was tired. I'd already given two tours. I knew I shouldn't take another person out, but Amy said her niece knew how to kayak and just needed a few pointers."

Gracie picked up his hand and caressed it.

"As soon as we got on the water, I knew her niece hadn't had lessons. The wind had picked up and the water was getting rough. I wanted us to return to shore. But her niece didn't listen to me."

Adam sucked in a big breath.

"The storm came in faster than I expected, and before I knew it, her kayak overturned, and Caitlin was caught in a rip current. I couldn't go into the rip current or I would get caught, too."

"She didn't make it out," Gracie said, her voice soft.

Adam shook his head. "I blamed myself and to numb the pain I drank. Once I started drinking, I couldn't stop. Every time I took a drink, I wanted more. My brothers held an intervention, and I went to rehab. I haven't had a drink for five years."

Gracie squeezed his hand. "I'm glad you're sober. And I'm glad you told me the story."

Adam turned and looked at Gracie. "I am, too." It felt like a weight had fallen off him. Something in the telling of the truth. Seth always told him that he needed to tell the truth. And he'd done it. He felt a pull toward

Gracie. Something that hadn't been there before. Something that he could call love. He trusted her with his biggest secret, a secret he believed made him untrustworthy. But she hadn't pushed him away, and she hadn't walked away. She'd offered him nothing but her support and love.

Adam moved closer to Gracie. He wanted to kiss her again. He wanted to feel her lips on his, her arms wrapped around him. His heart pounded but it felt like the right thing to do.

"Can I kiss you?"

Gracie nodded and her eyes filling with warmth.

Adam lowered his mouth to hers and wrapped his arms around her. The kiss was different this time. Softer. Gracie opened her mouth to him, and he dove in, tasting her lips, her mouth. She tasted like the scone they'd shared, and a warmth filled him. She wrapped her arms around him, and he pressed closer to her, his hands moving up and down her back, caressing her. He slipped his hands inside the jacket and kept moving them inside her layers of clothes until he reached her soft, bare skin. Her smell of lavender and something else, something that smelled musky and deep. Underneath his hands, she shivered and this time he knew it wasn't from the cold. A fire lit inside him and warmed him in a way he had never felt.

He felt like he might explode with the heat.

Max nudged at his palm and stuck his nose into Adam's jacket pocket. Adam removed his hands from Gracie and reached into his pocket. He gave Max a gentle nudge and handed Max a treat.

Gracie pulled away. She looked at her dog, smiling, and then back up at him. Her eyes were bright. "We should probably go before the tide comes in."

Adam slipped the book into the cave ledge, making sure it was hidden and not sticking out the way it had been when he'd found it.

"Let's go." Adam held out his hand and Gracie slipped hers into his.

Chapter 14

Gracie poured another cup of coffee and walked toward her office. She loved the early morning hours before anyone was up. Most mornings, she worked in the small space that she called her office. It was really just a large closet behind the front desk where she had set up a small desk and hung a couple pictures along the back wall. As she walked past the living room, she noticed a figure huddled in the corner of the couch. She stopped.

"Maddie?"

Gracie walked into the living room. Had something happened to Maddie? Did she break up with her boyfriend? Had he hut her? Why was she here this early? Did Maddie's mom, Lisa, know where she was this morning?

"Are you okay?" Gracie sat down on the couch beside her. Her heart pounded. "Does your mom know where you are?"

"I left a note for mom. I wanted to come over here. I feel safe over here with you and I know you'll understand." Tears rolled down her face.

"Are you hurt?"

"No," Maddie said. She looked up at Gracie. "I don't want to go to college next year."

"Oh." Gracie exhaled. "College can be a big decision. It can be hard to leave family."

"That's not it," Maddie said. "I want to take a year off."

"A gap year," Gracie said. She knew about gap years. In St. Louis, she'd hired a young woman as her assistant in her real estate office who was taking a year off. She needed to make money to travel. The last Gracie heard, she had never gone to college and was working as a ski instructor in Utah. College wasn't for everyone, and some people waited until they needed to pursue a specific career. There were many paths in life and Gracie never judged anyone's.

"Yes," Maddie said. "I love volunteering at the Wildlife Center, and I want to find other places with wildlife where I can work."

"You know the job market isn't very good right now for environmental jobs," Gracie said. She didn't want to discourage Maddie, but she wanted her to know the realistic picture.

"I know," Maddie said. "Uncle Sawyer and Uncle Bryan keep telling me I need to go to college and get a business degree. They said that's the only reliable job for me to have because I can always find a job in business."

"There is some truth to that," Gracie said, thinking of her own real estate license. She hadn't planned to be a real estate agent. But she drifted toward the career because of her love for homes. Once she'd gotten into the real estate track, she enjoyed finding just the right home for her clients. But something inside her had always known it was just a job. She loved her inn with a lot more passion than she had ever loved her real estate career. She hoped Maddie could find the same love for her career.

"But that's not what I want to do," Maddie said, her voice firm and strong. "I want to make a difference."

"You can make a difference in business," Gracie said. "You can serve on a board with your business skills and really make a difference to an environmental group." Gracie knew how much college meant to Maddie's family. She didn't want to steer her in a direction that would be harmful to her family who loved her and wanted the best for her.

Maddie shook her head. "There is something that comes alive inside of me when I am outdoors. Something wakes up, and I just want to stay there. I don't care if it's raining or cold. I love being outside."

Maddie's words rang in Gracie's head. She sounded like Adam. He loved the outdoors more than anything. He had gone to college and left after the first semester. He returned to Cranberry Bay and taken the state parks job and never looked back. "Have you talked to your Uncle Adam about this?" Gracie asked. "I think he would be someone good for you to talk to."

"I don't want to talk to him," Gracie said. "I'm afraid

he would say something to Uncle Bryan and Uncle Sawyer."

Gracie smiled. "Adam is very good at keeping confidences." She warmed thinking of their beach walk and the sharing of each other's stories.

Maddie nodded. "I will talk to him." She turned and hugged Gracie. "Thank you for your support. It really means a lot to me."

Gracie hugged Maddie in a close embrace. She felt like a daughter she might have had. Gracie loved being part of the small town community and finding family in the people who called Cranberry Bay home.

AFTER TALKING TO MADDIE, Gracie poured herself another cup of coffee. She opened the kitchen door and walked the garden footpath. The morning sun shone across the stones to the gazebo. Gracie removed a geranium from the flimsy black container. She scooped a small spot in the soil of the large pot with her hands and dropped the plant into the dirt. She covered the roots with soil, making sure not to cover up the other plants she'd strategically placed around the geranium. The large pots often looked like they held too many plants, but as the plants filled in and bloomed over the summer months, the pots became a cascade of colors.

"Gracie!" Katie pushed open the garden gate. Adam and Josh had fixed the latch, and now it swung easily. She carried a tray of pink and white geraniums. She wore a green canvas apron, and a small gardening shovel stuck out of one pocket. A pair of colorful flower gloves stuck out of a side pocket.

"I'm so glad you're here," Gracie said. "It's a perfect morning for planting flowers!"

Katie set the flowers onto one of the gazebo benches. "Where do I start?" She eyed the stack of empty pots.

Gracie pointed to a medium sized pot. "Why don't you start with that one?"

Katie walked to a row of empty pots. The pots framed the entryway to the gazebo and would make a perfect setting for Sasha and Greg, who would stand inside the gazebo with Paul, the long-time minister of the Cranberry Bay Community Church. The townspeople often joked that Paul had baptized everyone, married everyone, and given the final Celebration of Life for everyone.

Gracie had never been an active member of her church in St. Louis, attending only on Easter and Christmas with her parents and never with her ex-fiancé, who claimed religion was not for him.

Adam's face flashed in front of her mind. She hadn't been able to get him off her mind for the last two days, even though she hadn't seen him since their walk and kiss in the cave. But it wasn't just the kiss that was giving her a warm sensation. It was sharing her past with Adam and then him opening to her. Even though he was the first and only person in Cranberry Bay who she had told her story to, she didn't feel uncomfortable.

She'd never felt that way with her ex- fiancé. There

had always been a hint of danger, a hint of never being able to fully relax and let her guard down. Now she knew that had all been part of the abusive pattern. At the time, she had hoped that it would change, that at some point, with just a little more time, she would become comfortable with him, but it never happened. The edgy feeling always there, the need to keep her guard up.

"Gracie?" Katie stood beside her.

"Sorry." Gracie shook her head and pulled herself out of her thoughts.

"Is everything okay? I've been calling your name for the last few minutes, and you haven't heard me."

"Yes," Gracie said. "I'm just distracted with the wedding details. It's just a few weeks away."

"I know." Katie shook her head. "I feel the same way about the reception. Sawyer keeps trying to reassure me it will all come together." She smiled. "But it will all be worth it. I'm so happy to be able to do this for Sasha and Greg."

There was a loud clunk across the yard and Gracie whirled around. Sawyer stood beside Adam. The gate stood open as the two maneuvered a small riding lawn mower into the backyard.

"What are they doing?" Katie frowned as she placed her hands on her hips.

"The pavers." Gracie pointed to a large stack of stone pavers beside the back fence. "Adam said he needed to clear out the grasses and start over with fresh soil and then bark before he lays the pavers. It will keep the weeds down." Gracie kept her voice sure and steady.

"Mmmm…." Katie shook her head. "Well, as long as you know the plan, that's all that matters."

As long as she knew the plan. Gracie flushed. She knew the garden plan. They had been diligent about working on the map together, making sure the right plants were in the right places, and creating a timeline to make sure everything would bloom and be ready for the wedding. But did she know the plan of her relationship with Adam? Was there even a "them," or was it just a random kiss or two? How could there be a plan when Adam's first plan was to find a new job and move away?

She wanted him to be happy. But her life was in Cranberry Bay. She couldn't give up the inn and all of her friendships. Something inside her churned. It was more than that—she couldn't risk everything for love again. Even though she trusted Adam and knew he wasn't like her ex-fiancé, she couldn't take the leap and trust love again.

"You've got that look again." Katie picked up a small plant from the bench seat of the gazebo. "Something is the matter."

Gracie bit her lip. She wanted to tell Katie about Adam. It would help if her friend knew and she could talk to her about him. But now wasn't the time. Across the yard, Adam moved the lawn mower over a clump of grass. The morning sun heated the yard, and he'd removed his jacket. He wore a red t-shirt over faded blue jeans. His dark, curly hair framed his face. Gracie's stomach dove and nerves fluttered inside her. She felt like a high school girl with her first crush on what would become her first boyfriend.

"It's Adam, isn't it?" Katie peered at Adam. "Something happened with you two."

"How did you know?" Gracie asked, her face flushed. She was so used to not talking about her past and what happened with her ex-fiancé that it felt unnatural and strained to talk about her feelings with Adam.

Katie shrugged and smiled. "Call it intuition. Come on." She walked to the seat and patted it with her hand. "Let's talk."

"Not here." Gracie picked up another package of petunias. "We will be too obvious."

"You're right," Katie said. "I don't know why I didn't think of that. It wasn't that long ago that I didn't know what to do with my feelings about Sawyer! Let's keep working. We can plant and talk, and no one will suspect a thing."

Katie picked up three packages of flowers. She balanced them in her left hand and grabbed a small hand rake. "There are a couple more pots in the back of the gazebo for us to fill."

Gracie picked up a bag of soil and followed Katie to the back of the gazebo. She sat down on the bench and leaned over to open the soil bag. "I don't know where to begin," she said, her voice soft.

"At the beginning is always the best place," Katie said, her voice light and filled with joy. "You know we all love Adam and want to see him happy. You two have been friends for a while. I'm not surprised there are feelings."

"I guess I am," Gracie said. "I just didn't really plan for my feelings to be anything more than friendship."

"You can never plan for these things," Katie said. "Rylee, Ivy, myself, and now Sasha. All of us would tell you that you can't plan love. When love hits it hits. The only plan you can make is to surrender."

"But he's moving," Gracie said, her voice choked with emotion. "How can I even think about falling in love with him when he's moving?"

"You could go with him," Katie said, her voice quiet. "I know you love the inn and it's been your safe place since you moved here. But sometimes you have to let go of those things that are familiar. And," Katie paused. "You could aways open an inn in Montana."

The tears swelled in Gracie's throat. A part of her knew that what Katie said made perfect sense. She loved her inn. But she could run an inn in Montana, too. Her feelings were asking her to take a chance, step into what would be different. The New Leaf Inn in Cranberry Bay had asked her to take a chance, but it was a different way of taking chances. All the chances depended on her own abilities and resources. She didn't have to trust anyone but herself. The thought of trusting someone else scared her, even if that person was Adam.

"Sometimes," Katie said, "I like to play the What If game."

"The What If game?" Gracie asked.

"I like to place myself a little bit in the future and ask

myself, what if I didn't make that choice? What would my life be like?"

Gracie nodded. She played the What If game, too, but it was usually more about her fears and worries.

Now, she pictured herself in the fall. The tide would be low, and Max would be walking by her side. There would be tide pools along the rocky shore. It would be like it had been a few mornings ago. But Adam would be gone. She would be alone. He wouldn't be there to surprise her with coffee, or have treats in his pocket for Max. She would finish her walk, return to the inn, and her life would be filled with the same things it was now—running the inn, attending event meetings for Cranberry Bay, and listening to each of her friends talk about the love and joy they felt in their marriages. Eventually, there might be a few dates, maybe in Pelican Shores. But it wouldn't be Adam. She wouldn't have that ease and familiarity of friendship which had deepened into so much more.

A shadow crossed the gazebo. She looked up to find Adam standing in front of her, gazing at her with warmth. "I'm going to head up to Sasha's bakery and grab some things for lunch. Would you like a turkey sandwich?"

Gracie warmed. Adam always remembered what she liked, from the type of sandwich she preferred to how she liked her coffee to the small treats he kept in his pocket for Max. He noticed all the details because he cared about her.

"Yes," Gracie said. "I would like a turkey sandwich."

"What would you like?" Adam turned to Katie. "I'm taking orders."

"I'm going to grab lunch with Sawyer," Katie said. "He's got a meeting in Pelican Shores early this afternoon and we'll get lunch at the Dockshore. Best clam chowder around!"

Adam turned back to Gracie. His ears reddened. "I have time this afternoon to finish up the pavers and then we can fill in the spots that look empty with some lavender. I've got extra plants in the truck that I picked up yesterday."

"That would be perfect," Gracie said. Her heart expanded. She felt so happy when she was around Adam. How had she not noticed the feelings developing? It seemed so obvious to her now.

Adam ducked out of the gazebo and headed across the lawn to the open gate. Gracie turned to find Katie wiping her hands on her pants. She smiled at Gracie. "Sometimes it just takes seeing what you have by picturing what it would be like without it."

Katie stepped out of the gazebo and walked toward Sawyer as Gracie picked up the last plant in the plastic container. She cleared a small space along the edges where the white flowers would drape over the rims of the pot as it bloomed, creating a cascade of flowers that resembled a small waterfall. She felt happier than she had in a long time, and that happiness came from the bubbling emotions inside her about Adam.

Chapter 15

Adam waited for Sasha to put the turkey croissant sandwich into one of the bakery's white bags. The bakery's emblem swirled across the front of the bag, thick lines curled around in a circle and the shape of the bay. Katie and Sasha had designed the logo a couple years ago to help Sasha differentiate her bakery from the one in Sea Shore Cove, who used simple white bags for their bakery items.

"Here's your tea." Sasha pushed two to-go cups with tea bag strings hanging over the edge toward Adam. "How is everything going at the inn? I really appreciate Gracie hosting our wedding."

"We're going to make it in time," Adam said. "Everything has really come together over the last couple days."

Sasha leaned toward him. "Greg and I are so happy that you are the Best Man with Gracie as the Maid of Honor."

Adam couldn't hold back the grin that broke across his face.

"Mmmm…" Sasha said. "I think I know this look. I've seen it on a few others recently." She raised her hand and ticked off on her fingers. "Ivy. Josh. Katie. Sawyer. Rylee. Bryan."

Adam shrugged. "I don't know what you're talking about. I'm just really happy for you and Greg."

Sasha rolled her eyes and smiled at him. "It's okay if you don't want to admit you have feelings for Gracie. All of us understand falling in love."

Adam's face warmed. His phone buzzed against his leg. "Gotta go."

He balanced the to-go tray with the bag holding the two sandwiches and headed toward his truck. By the time he reached his truck, the call had gone to voicemail. He put the to-go tray on the floor and set the sandwiches on the passenger seat. Reaching into his pocket, he pulled out his phone and punched the voice mail button.

"Adam!" Drew's voice boomed. "Can you give us a call as soon as possible?"

Adam took a deep breath. He wanted this job. It was a perfect fit for him. His heart pounded as he punched in William's number.

"Adam!" William said. "We'd like to offer you the job. As the job listing stated, you've got full benefits, and we'll get you set up with housing. Of course, you'll probably want to purchase your own property, but we have a home to offer you until you do."

Adam inhaled. He had landed not only a job where

he could grow and expand, but one that came with housing. He wouldn't have to live in a trailer and the salary was high enough with advancement each year, he could eventually buy his own home.

"When do I start?" Adam asked.

"We'd like you here as soon as you can get here," William said. "We have a City Council meeting next Wednesday. It'd be great if you could make that."

Adam mentally calculated. The wedding was this weekend. He would need to do a few things Monday but could leave by Tuesday. "If I drive straight through, I should be there by Wednesday night for the meeting."

"Great," William said. "We'll get you on the agenda and introduce you. Congratulations. We're all so happy you'll be joining us. You were our top candidate."

Adam's chest expanded. He got the job. A small part of him had worried that the kayak accident might cause some concern. He wasn't applying for a job that would ask him to give kayak lessons or be responsible for someone, but it didn't matter. People did their own research and made their own judgments. Anything could be found by doing a Google search.

He headed toward a small row of townhouses lining the river. He needed to gather his thoughts. He sat on a bench at the park and stared at the river. He'd lived in this town his whole life. His family. His brothers. His Dad. His Mom. They were all still here.

He had amazing memories from fishing in the bay to helping out with the Christmas tree lights each year to loading the canned goods on the fire truck during Soup

for Santa. In the last couple years, the downtown businesses had banded together for the July 4th Festival, the
holiday lights competition, and the fall harvest celebration.

He was excited about this job. He knew it would be
an opportunity to use the skills he'd developed with the
Wildlife Center. But his feelings for Gracie were
confusing everything. How could he leave her? He felt so
alive and happy when they were together. But at the same
time, the guilt from the accident trapped him. How could
he ever protect someone he loved in his care? How could
he protect Gracie as a husband?

For years, Adam had carried his secret in his heart.
The inability to rescue someone under his care. He had
guarded the truth close to him, unwilling to let anyone
in, even Seth, his AA sponsor, barely scratched the
surface of how he felt about the event. The event he
never wanted to talk about. The event that made him
sure he could never protect another person. But he
opened up to Gracie and she hadn't judged him. She
hadn't walked away. And she had told him about her
past.

"Uncle Adam." Maddie rode her bike up to the
bench where he sat looking over the river.

"Maddie!" Adam said. He was always glad to see his
niece. He knew it had been stressful for her with the pressure from both Sawyer and Bryan about her college decision. She'd been quiet about which college she was going
to choose, although she told them she'd gotten accepted
to both.

"Want to join me?" He asked and patted the bench beside him.

"I do," Maddie said, her face lit up with a big smile.

She sat down beside him and kicked her legs out in front of her. "I want to talk to you. I want to tell you something and Gracie said you are a good confident."

Adam flushed at the positive compliment. "I don't talk about what people tell me."

"I want to take a gap year," Maddie said. She fiddled with a small strap on her bike.

Adam nodded. It didn't surprise him that Maddie didn't want to go straight to college. She had a rough start to high school, though she regained her footing in Cranberry Bay. But she hadn't been as excited for college as Sawyer, Bryan, and her mom, Lisa, were. Adam never liked to interfere in family conflict, and without children of his own, he often felt like he didn't have the right to tell Sawyer or Lisa how to raise their children. But he watched Maddie and saw her conflicted emotions every time her college decision came up. He was glad she was confiding in him now.

"It can be good to wait for college," Adam said. "Probably something I should have done. I knew I didn't want to get a four-year degree, but it was what was expected."

"That's how I feel," Maddie said. "Bryan, Sawyer, and Mom all expect me to go to college. But that's not what I want."

"What do you want, Maddie?" Adam asked.

"I want to work in the outdoors, like you," Maddie

said. "There is something about the outdoors. I just come alive. I know it's not a good time for outdoor jobs and there are budget cuts."

"Yes," Adam said. "It isn't the best time. But there may never be a best time, and you can't do something that your heart isn't calling you to do."

He paused. He knew what his heart was telling him to do with his job, but what about Gracie? What was his heart telling him to do about Gracie? Could he override his fears about his past and trust that he could protect her?

"The Wildlife Center needs someone to help out," Maddie said. "I could stay in Cranberry Bay and help out. But I'm worried about telling Uncle Sawyer, Uncle Bryan, and Mom. They want me to be perfect. They will see this as too much of who I used to be. A failure. I don't want to be labeled like that." Maddie bit her lower lip.

"Mmmm…" Adam said. "You could volunteer at the Wildlife Center." He paused.

"But…" Maddie pressed him.

"But it's also good to get experience in other places. I just got the job at the Environmental Center in Montana. I might need an intern."

"Really?" Maddie's face lit up.

"I would need to check first," Adam said. "But I don't know why not. I've been hired as the director and I'm sure I'm going to need lots of help getting the place off the ground. I don't know the budget yet, but as an intern, you would be working for experience and maybe a small stipend. There is housing but I plan to buy my own house, a big house with enough rooms for everyone to visit. I would have room for you."

"This is so perfect!" Maddie said.

"You're going to have to tell your mom and uncles about your gap year. But it might make it easier if they knew you were going to come with me."

"It will make it a lot easier!" Maddie jumped up and threw her arms around him. "Thank you Uncle Adam!" She waved and danced out the door.

His phone buzzed. He saw it was a text from Gracie. *Everything okay? Did you get the sandwiches?*

Yes, Adam texted. *Be right there.* He stood. Seth always said to do the next indicated thing. The next thing for him was to bring lunch to Gracie. He still had a week. A week with a wedding where he and Gracie would stand together as Sasha and Greg got married. And maybe in that week, he could find the courage Maddie had and tell Gracie how he felt about her and ask her to join him in Montana.

Chapter 16

Gracie smoothed her hands over the green silk dress. It fell to her knees and swirled out in a gentle swish around her legs. The early evening sun shone through the windows of her bedroom. She slipped on her cream-colored sandals. That afternoon, she'd gone with everyone to get their nails done in Pelican Shores. Sasha had said it was her treat.

Greg was treating Bryan, Adam, Sawyer, and Josh to a round of golf at the Pelican Shores golf course. Gracie and Sasha had raised their eyebrows when Greg announced it. Sawyer and Bryan often played golf and took potential investors up and down the coast to some of the best golf courses. Josh played in low-key games, usually ones that raised money for the schools. But neither one of them had ever heard or seen Adam pick up a club.

Aunt Celia bustled into the room. She carried a handful of bracelets, necklaces, and earrings. "I just couldn't decide which one would go best with your dress."

Gracie swallowed the tears that were gathering in her throat. She'd played dress up with Aunt Celia's jewelry when she was a child. Aunt Celia would keep a bag of clothes tucked into the back of her closet and Gracie loved to try on all the long swirling skirts, dangling scarfs, and the costume jewelry.

"How about this one?" Gracie leaned over and lifted a simple green glass pendant on a long chain.

"That's one of my favorites," Aunt Celia said. "I got it at an art sale when I took a little tour around the San Juan Islands in Washington State."

Gracie envied her aunt's ability to go wherever she wanted. She'd never seemed to have any fears about traveling and was just as comfortable traveling alone as she was traveling in a tour group. Gracie longed to be a little more adventurous herself, but something inside her always stopped the adventure of trading the familiar for the unfamiliar. Cranberry Bay and the New Leaf Inn had been her biggest adventure.

Aunt Celia took the necklace and dropped it over Gracie's head. Gracie lifted her hair and Aunt Celia fastened the jewelry in place. She stepped to the front of Gracie and smiled at her. "You look beautiful, darling."

"So do you," Gracie said.

Her aunt's face softened. "I feel so relaxed in Cranberry Bay. It's such a charming small town and…." She trailed off.

Gracie peered at her aunt. "Is everything okay? Your health?"

"Yes, dear, my health is fine." Aunt Celia's voice dropped. "I made a bad financial deal. I invested in a start-up company with a friend's daughter. It's been very stressful. My lawyer is trying to recoup the money, but it looks like I will have to sell quite a bit."

"Your home?" Gracie couldn't imagine her aunt living anywhere other than her sprawling home overlooking a park.

"Unfortunately, it seems that way," Aunt Celia said. She smiled. But her smile didn't reach her eyes. "I probably needed to downsize, but this wasn't the way I saw it happening."

"Is there anything I can do?" Gracie asked. She had used most of her savings on the New Leaf Inn, but she could take out a loan if needed to help her aunt get a new home.

Downstairs, the bell above the front door chimed, announcing someone's arrival. Adam's voice called out. "Gracie! Hello."

"Let's not worry about it right now." Aunt Celia patted her arm. "We have a wedding to go to."

Gracie's heart gave a little flutter. They were driving over to a restaurant in Sea Shore Cove for the rehearsal dinner. There wasn't actually going to be a rehearsal, but Greg insisted on treating all of them to a beautiful dinner at one restaurant with the best view on the coast.

"Thank you for the jewelry." Gracie reached out and hugged her aunt. "And for keeping an eye on the inn tonight. I think most of the guests are checked in, but there is one couple who hasn't arrived yet. Please call me if you have any problems."

"Don't worry dear." Aunt Celia waved her hand in front of her face. "I have everything under control here. Go enjoy yourself." She leaned forward and kissed Gracie's cheek.

As Gracie descended the staircase, Adam looked up at her. Their eyes met and her stomach danced. Adam wore a white dress shirt, khaki pants, and a suit coat with a green tie that matched her dress. She had only seen Adam dressed in a suit and tie a handful of times but she never remembered feeling this flustered.

"You look beautiful." Adam held out his hand as she descended the last stair.

Gracie slipped hers into his. "You look pretty good yourself."

He squeezed her hand.

Adam opened the door and escorted her outside to his truck. He'd parked along the sidewalk in the ten-minute unloading zone. He opened the door for her, and she slipped inside. The warm, familiar scent of Adam filled the truck. It swirled around her and made her body fill with a longing she couldn't escape. A longing for Adam, his mouth on hers, his arms around her, pulling her close, protecting her, and loving her.

She leaned over and unlocked the driver's door. He opened it and climbed inside.

Adam drove toward Sea Shore Cove but instead of

turning toward the row of restaurants lining the shore-line, he turned left and up to the state park.

"Where are we going?" Gracie asked. "We're going to be late." She hated being late anywhere, but especially for Sasha and Greg's special dinner.

"It's okay," Adam said. "I told Greg we would be a few minutes late. I have something to tell you."

Gracie's heart pounded as Adam pulled up the windy, narrow road leading to the overlook. A handful of cars were already parked, waiting to watch the sunset, even though it wouldn't happen for another hour or so.

Adam pulled into an open parking space and turned off the truck. He turned to face her. His eyes were dark and serious. "Gracie."

"You got the job," Gracie said, her voice soft and quiet.

"Yes," Adam said. "They are offering me a full package with benefits."

"I'm happy for you." Gracie forced the feelings inside her to settle. She wanted the best for him. And the best thing for him was his new job. He was leaving Cranberry Bay. Her chest constricted and her throat closed. She felt the tears gathering. He was leaving.

"They want me to go next week," Adam said. "I'll be in the wedding, and then I'll leave. Maddie wants to come, too."

"She talked to you," Gracie said. She struggled to keep her composure. "I suggested she might find an ally in you about her college decision."

Adam nodded. "She did. I love both my brothers, and I don't want to disrespect them or their wishes for Maddie. But I understand Maddie. I understand that struggle of wanting to go somewhere that is bigger than you, not in a classroom, but in the outdoors with your hands getting dirty and your feet getting wet."

Gracie loved Adam's passion. She loved his passion for the work he did, for the way he moved in the world, rescuing birds and repairing trails. The last thing she ever wanted to do was stand in the way of that passion or give him any discouragement for following his passion. Even if that meant letting him go.

"I'm really happy for you," she said, and she knew that she meant it. She loved Adam. She wanted the best for him and this was the best. He'd gotten a job where he could continue to work outdoors and build something around what he loved.

"I want you to come with me," Adam said, his voice low and deep.

"To Montana?" Gracie asked. She swallowed hard. Adam wanted her to go to Montana with him. Her heart lifted with what she could only describe as hope, a feeling of warmth so deep it cascaded all the way to her toes.

"Yes," Adam said. "I want you to move with me."

"Move with you?" Gracie swallowed. The hope died inside her. Adam hadn't asked her to marry him. He wanted her to move with him, as a friend, a pal. He was keeping the pact they'd made to each other. Just friends. Maybe friends who kissed a little, but they were just friends. They'd both agreed that marriage wasn't for them. But something inside her had changed. She wanted what her friends had. She wanted the companionship, waking up with the same person in the morning, the shared coffee and talks, the late-night talks, and all the ways they came together during the day. She wanted more than their original pact of friendship. She wanted so much more.

Gracie inhaled as both her and Adam's phone beeped at the same time. Grateful to the distraction, she read the text from Sasha. *Where are you? We are waiting for you before we start dinner.*

"The dinner," Gracie said as she slid her phone back into her purse.

Adam started the truck and silence filled the truck.

Gracie stared out the window. She remembered Katie telling her to play the What If game. In her What If game, she saw herself on the beach below them now, walking by herself, without Adam, Max running at her side. It wasn't a horrible image, but something was missing. Something inside her was missing. Adam. But she couldn't go to Montana as his friend. Her feelings had deepened to much more than friendship and it didn't seem like Adam wanted to offer her anything more.

"It's okay," Adam said, his voice soft. "I know this is a big decision."

Gracie nodded. She loved him. She knew she loved him. But he had to love her, too. He wasn't asking her to marry him. He was asking her to come with him and it wasn't enough. She needed more. She needed to know that he loved her the way she knew she loved him. She needed the commitment she thought she'd never want again—marriage.

Chapter 17

The sun sank toward the Pacific Ocean outside the long windows framing the restaurant. Greg had reserved the best table in the room, and they had a full view of the pending sunset.

Adam picked at his salad with his fork. His stomach churned. He drizzled more dressing onto the lettuce, the leaves wilting with the weight of the liquid.

"Do you have enough salad for that dressing?" Maddie leaned over and pointed to his salad.

"Guess I wasn't paying attention." Adam poked his fork into the lettuce and dropped it onto her plate.

"Gross." Maddie wrinkled her nose.

"Maddie!" Sawyer boomed from the other end of the table. "Have you made your decision about which college you are going to attend?"

Maddie froze, her fork halfway to her plate. She dropped it as all eyes at the table turned to her.

"Tell us," Bryan said. "Will it be the Ducks or the Huskies?"

"We'll cheer for either and be happy for you," Lisa said, her eyes beaming at Maddie. "I'm so proud of you and all the hard work you've done."

"Why is this about me?" Maddie muttered under her breath. "It's a rehearsal dinner for Sasha and Greg."

"Do you want me to say something?" Adam asked, his voice quiet and soft.

"No," Maddie said. She pushed back her chair and stood. "I've decided."

"Tell us!" Sawyer clapped his hands. His eyes beamed with pride. "I know you're going to be a Husky.

"I'm not going to either school."

Silence filled the table.

"Have you been accepted somewhere else, dear?" Rebecca Shuster smiled at Maddie.

"No," Maddie said. "I'm taking a gap year."

"A what?" Rebecca said. "I'm sorry, I don't know the lingo of you kids today."

"A gap year, Mom," Lisa said, her voice tight and strained. "It's when someone takes a year off between high school and college to find themselves."

"Where did you lose yourself?" Lauren, Sawyer's eleven-year-old daughter asked. "Do you want us to help you look for her?"

Maddie giggled. "I'm right here," she said. "But I'm going to delay college for a year."

"What will you do?" Sasha asked.

"I thought about staying in Cranberry Bay and

volunteering at the Wildlife Center," Maddie said. "But I talked to Adam."

Adam nodded.

"And he said he'll need an intern in his new job."

"You got the job!" Bryan stood and raised his glass. "This deserves a toast!"

Adam ducked his head. He wasn't used to this much attention on him as congratulations filled the air.

"When do you leave?" Sawyer asked.

"Tuesday," Adam said. "I'll stay for the wedding this weekend, then pack Monday, and head out on Tuesday."

"So soon," Rebecca said, tears pooling in her eyes. "But I'm so happy for you. This is a wonderful opportunity." Rebeca turned to Adam. "I couldn't be prouder of you."

Emotion overwhelmed Adam. He was leaving. He was leaving all the people at this table who'd supported him and loved him throughout his life. The people who meant the most to him.

Maddie turned and smiled at him. "I'm so happy I get to come with you."

Adam nodded at her. Maddie coming with him would help with leaving everyone behind.

Adam took a sip of his water. He peered at Gracie over his glass. The biggest loss was Gracie. She hadn't given him any sign that she wanted to join him. And now, the look on her face was a mixture of sadness, joy, and something unreadable. Something that seemed like she'd tucked a part of herself that had just begun to emerge back away in a deep, dark spot where no one could reach her. Especially not him.

———

THE NEXT MORNING, Adam pulled his truck into the Wildlife Center parking lot. The parking lot had a handful of cars, and he recognized all of them. The five members of the board and Bill, the veterinarian who helped with the injured birds. It looked like the first interview candidate for the director position hadn't arrived yet.

Adam shut the truck off. He opened the door, grabbed his bag, and headed inside.

"Morning, Adam!" Angie greeted him. She held a Western Seagull that squeaked loudly. "Just stop your talking to me." She scolded the bird.

"How is our puffin patient?" Adam peered into the crate near the front door.

"Doing great!" Angie said. "We should be ready to release the bird any day."

"I'm leaving on Tuesday but would like to be part of the release, if possible," Adam said. He hoped Gracie would be there. But after last night, he wasn't sure. She'd been supportive about his job offer, but once they'd gotten to the dinner, Gracie had slipped past him to sit beside Rylee. She'd ridden home with Rylee and Bryan and avoided him. Was this her way of telling him she wouldn't join him? That she didn't want to consider it? And that he'd been wrong about his feelings?

A pit of darkness formed in his mind. When was the last time he went to an AA meeting? He couldn't remember. Maybe a week? He'd gotten so busy with the garden and preparing for the wedding that his regular schedule had slipped away.

He knew it was a big decision for Gracie to go with him, but he hoped she would have said something by the end of the night. Instead, she had grown more and more distant as the night went on. The worst had been she politely declined his offer to take her home. Adam checked his messages multiple times during the night, but there was nothing from her and there was nothing from her this morning, either.

"I set us up in the back room," Angie said. She frowned. "It's a little tight with all of us at the table."

Adam strode into the backroom. The other members of the board sat around the table, their chairs pushed close together. A single chair sat at the head of the table, and three chairs remained open. One for him, Angie, and Bill.

"We'll make it work," Adam said. "Our candidate might as well know what he's getting into."

"She," Angie said, and smiled. "Our first candidate is Lisa Jackson."

"From the Sea Stack Environmental program?" Adam asked. Lisa had run that program for over twenty-five years. He was surprised she would want to apply for the director position and drop to part-time.

"Yes," Angie said and lowered her voice. "She wants a change."

"Does she know it's part-time?" Adam asked.

"I assume so," Angie said. "The position said part-time when we posted it."

Adam nodded and sat down. Lisa would be an excellent director. She had a keen understanding of the Wildlife Center and the birds they served. Angie placed the list of interview questions in front of all the board members.

"She's here," Angie said and pointed toward a silver car that just parked outside the window.

Bill pulled out a chair and took the seat beside Adam. Angie waited for a minute and when Lisa appeared in the doorway, she waved, smiled, and ushered her in.

"I think you know everyone," Angie said. "We're happy you applied for the position."

"I am, too," Lisa said and smiled. She wore khaki pants, a simple cream blouse, and her hair curled around her oval face.

The interview lasted over an hour. It was easy to talk to Lisa. She'd been rescuing stranded birds in the Sea Shore Cove program for years and was passionate and dedicated to her job of environmental stewardship. By the end of the hour, the board had a quick conference and offered her the job with a start date as soon as she could give notice to her current job.

After Lisa left, Bill said, "You know Lisa's job is open now. It's full time."

Adam nodded. "They've got a qualified woman who will likely step in and take the position. She's been acting as the assistant to Lisa for a couple years now."

"Just hoping you might be persuaded to stay," Bill said. "You're leaving a big hole here."

"Thanks." Adam swallowed hard. The Wildlife Center had been his passion. It had seen him through his early years of sobriety. But he couldn't see himself working in the Sea Shore Cove Program. He'd never felt called to be on the beach the way that job demanded.

"Looks like the release date for the puffin will be on Monday." Angie pointed to the open date on the large calendar hanging on the wall beside a stack of empty crates.

"Monday is perfect." Monday would be the day before he needed to leave. It was the perfect day to release the puffin.

But something inside Adam churned. Feelings he hadn't allowed himself to feel. He'd never been good at feelings. The alcohol had always taken away his feelings of sadness over not only what had happened in the kayak accident, but also the shame that built up with each drink he drank. He promised himself each time he wouldn't drink again, but something wouldn't let him keep that promise. For a while he could control it. He could drink hard the night before and still meet his obligations. But after the kayak accident, something inside him fell apart. He couldn't control the urge to drink, the need to not feel the guilt and remorse, and once he started drinking, he couldn't stop.

"Better go," Adam said. He needed to keep busy. Busy so he didn't think about having a drink and numbing his emotions. "I've got some things to take care of."

"See you Monday," Angie said.

Adam walked to his truck. No matter how he tried to push them aside with positive affirmations, the AA slogans of *Keep it Simple* and *One Day at A Time*, his feelings flooded him. Gracie and her distance. Gracie and her silent rejection of his offer. His emotions over leaving Cranberry Bay. He took a deep breath. *One Day at a Time. One Minute at a Time.* But he couldn't push the urge aside. He wanted a drink.

Adam inserted his key into the truck before driving out of the parking lot. He turned the vehicle onto the coastal highway. The feeling pounded in him. One drink or maybe two, and it would take away the feelings inside him. He could do it. No one would ever know. He could stop by the store, pick up a pack of beer. Beer didn't get him that drunk. He needed to pick up a few things for dinner anyway.

The thoughts whirled in his head, filling his mind pushing the feelings higher. The need to drink. The thought of the beer sliding down his throat. It would take away all the feelings he was having about leaving and Gracie. The craving overwhelmed his senses. It was all he could think about.

Adam pulled into the supermarket parking lot. He parked his truck and stopped. He shouldn't buy some-thing at the supermarket in Sea Shore Cove. What if someone from his AA meetings was here? He'd heard the stories all the time. The men who wanted a drink but then ran into someone from an AA meeting, and they hauled them off to a meeting. He didn't want that. Not now. Not today. He wanted a drink.

Adam eyed the liquor store across the street. It would be easier. He could pick up a bottle of scotch. It was early in the day. He wouldn't run into anyone that might haul him off to an AA meeting. He inserted his keys back into his truck and pulled out of the parking lot. In minutes he was in front of the liquor store. No one would ever know, and it would be just this once. His mood buoyed by the hope of that first drink, sliding down his throat and taking away all his conflicted emotions.

Chapter 18

On Saturday morning, Gracie adjusted her dress. She stood in the inn's largest bedroom, the one she named the Lilac Suite. The heart-scooped neckline curved and dropped to a skirt that swung above her knees. She padded across the room to Sasha, who stood in front of the full-length mirror. Jill, Cranberry Bay's best hairdresser, pinned a small strand of Sasha's hair into the pearl clip which held the rest of Sasha's hair above her neck. Long beaded earrings dangled from her ears.

"You look wonderful," Gracie said.

"So do you." Sasha smiled. "Thank you for being my Maid of Honor."

Gracie took Sasha's hand and squeezed.

A loud crash sounded in the room next door, and Greg's voice boomed out, "Nothing broke!"

Sasha grinned. Greg and Adam were getting ready in the room next to them. Gracie peered out of the thick, heavy curtains. The room overlooked the garden area which was now blooming with purples, pinks, and yellow flowers. Two rows of white chairs sat in front of the gazebo. The sun streamed through the gazebo and across the garden. The weather couldn't have been more perfect for a wedding. A light breeze blew from the bay, and there wasn't a drop of rain in the forecast.

"You haven't said much about Adam's new job." Sasha turned to Gracie.

Jill busied herself at the small table where she'd set up all of her products and sprays, clips, and cutting scissors. Hair stylists were in high demand in the small coastal towns and Jill was one of the best. She kept the secrets poured out to her while the women were receiving cuts and colors.

"I'm happy for him," Gracie said, knowing that whatever she said about Adam would be held in confidence by Jill.

"And…." Sasha leaned closer to her.

Gracie raised her hands in the air and lowered her voice. "He asked me to go with him."

"And you said yes!" Sasha's voice rose in excitement.

"I haven't given him an answer yet." Gracie stared at the floor, her emotions churning. She hadn't given Adam an answer because she didn't just want to go with him. She wanted a commitment, a lifetime commitment. She wanted what both of them had sworn they wouldn't ever want from each other.

"What's holding you back?" Sasha lowered his voice

and touched Gracie's arm. "Are you scared to go with him? You love him, right?"

Tears pooled in the corners of Gracie's eyes. She did love Adam. She wasn't sure when it had happened, but she loved him. All of him. But did he love her? He hadn't asked her to go with him and marry him. He'd asked her to go with him because they were friends who had kissed. "I can't just go with him. I need more. I need a commitment."

Sasha sat down in the small chair in front of the mirror. "You know I never thought I would see Greg again, and when we did run into each other, the last thing I wanted was to have him sweep in and buy my love."

Gracie nodded. She remembered the struggle Sasha went through. She had been running her bakery on her own for so long and raising Tyler. They'd watched her gradually surrender to Greg and to love.

"But now," Sasha said, her cheeks flushed, "I'm so glad I surrendered and took the chance. I couldn't imagine my life without him. Talk to Adam. Tell him how you feel."

Gracie swallowed the lump in her throat. She knew Sasha was right. She needed to talk to Adam. She couldn't just leave him without an answer. But what would he say when she told him she needed more? Would she lose their friendship because she was asking for more? If she didn't say anything and stayed in Cranberry Bay, she could always remain friends with Adam. She would see him when he returned home for the Shuster Christmas holidays.

But something twisted inside her. What if he didn't return home? What if he stayed in Montana and everyone flew out to see him? She would be alone. Sasha, Greg, and Tyler had already announced they planned to go to Hawaii for Christmas. Ivy and Josh had their new baby and would celebrate Christmas at Josh's home. Katie, Sawyer, Rylee, and Bryan would all go to Montana. Of course, he would invite her, but he would ask her as his friend? And would that be enough? Her heart felt conflicted. She didn't think it would be. No, she corrected herself. She knew it wouldn't be. She wanted more. She wanted the commitment of forever with Adam.

"Sasha! Gracie!" Aunt Celia said as she knocked on the door. She pushed open the bedroom door. "It's about time." She inhaled. "You both look stunning."

"Thank you." Sasha twirled, and her dress flared around her.

"Everyone is gathered in the garden." She turned to Gracie. "Adam and Greg are waiting at the gazebo."

Gracie peered through the small slit in the curtain. Adam stood beside Greg. He wore a black tux with a polka dot bow tie that matched the color of her dress.

Aunt Celia stepped back into the room, a large bouquet of flowers in her hands this time.

Sasha took the flowers. "Ready?" She turned to Gracie.

Adam looked up at the window and Gracie stepped back out of view. "Yes."

Gracie's heart pounded as if it were her own

wedding. A wedding she believed she never wanted, but now she knew she did and with whom. She followed Sasha down the stairs and out the front doorway. They'd agreed to use the front door then go in through the open gate and walk down the stone pathway up to the gazebo.

A pair of musicians from Sea Shore Cove played the entrance of Cannon in D. Gracie stepped along the pathway and walked past Rylee, who had Max by her side on a leash and Bryan, Josh, Ivy, and their daughter, who Ivy held in her lap. Sawyer and Katie, Aunt Celia and Rebecca Shuster who sat with Jack, the town lawyer and longtime family friend. It was just as Sasha had requested. Family and closest friends. The part of Cranberry Bay that made Cranberry Bay home to Gracie.

She kept her eyes focused on the gazebo and Paul, the Community Church minister, who stood at the front and would read the wedding ceremony. When she got to the front of the gazebo, she looked up at Adam. His eyes sparkled at her. Her heart pounded. She inhaled. She knew he cared about her, but did he love her enough to make that final commitment? The one they both had sworn they didn't want?

The wedding march started and everyone rose.

Sasha made her way down the path and stopped next to Greg.

"Good afternoon!" Minister Paul said. "We are gathered here today to celebrate the marriage of Sasha and Greg."

The words poured over Gracie. They were words she was supposed to hear during the wedding with her ex-fiancé. But they would have been all wrong. She knew that now. Marriage wasn't supposed to be filled with fear. It was supposed to be a partnership. One where two people could come together and be more than they were on their own, supporting each other through life's storms and joys.

She looked at her friends gathered around them. Each of them had found their true love, and all of them had taken a risk on that love. Could she take that same risk and tell Adam how she felt and what she needed from him? Did he feel the same?

The words of the vows Greg and Sasha had written themselves washed over her. Love. Companionship. Protection. Tenderness. Friendship.

The things she had with Adam.

"And you may now kiss the bride," Minister Paul said.

Sasha and Greg leaned close together and as they kissed each other, Gracie looked up into Adam's eyes. A shadow crossed his face, and something in her tightened.

Chapter 19

Adam walked beside Gracie as they followed Sasha and Greg down the path. He couldn't fight the emotions crashing inside him. The way Gracie looked at him, the feelings. It was more intense than anything he'd known. He needed a drink. Not later. Now.

Outside the inn, the old Studebaker cars sat waiting to take Sasha and Greg to the reception at Katie's barn. Another one sat behind it, larger, with room for him, Gracie, Rylee, and Bryan. Ivy and Josh had insisted they'd drive in their own car, and Jack wanted to drive Rebecca in his new Subaru. Katie and Sawyer got into Sawyer's Audi, and Sawyer had grinned sheepishly. "I just like my own car."

"I'll meet you over there," Adam said. "I'm going to drive my truck." The urge inside of him to get to that bottle, and have one drink, just one. It would settle him. He would enjoy the reception. And no one would know.

Rylee hopped into the backseat of the Studebaker. "Come on." She patted the seat.

Bryan stepped away from the car and toward Adam. "What's going on?"

"Nothing," Adam said. "I just wanted to drive my own truck."

"Come on, man." Bryan put his hand on Adam's shoulder. "We're all riding in the car over here."

Adam couldn't resist. He couldn't walk away and insist he drive his own car without looking suspicious. And that was the last thing he wanted. His brothers loved him, and he couldn't let them know he was going to have a drink. The ability to lie for his drink moved over him quickly, the way it always did.

Adam slipped into the car beside Rylee. She moved over so he was beside Gracie. Their legs pressed together. The driver, a tall man who Greg had hired, pulled the car away from the inn and drove toward Katie and Sawyer's home.

"That was a beautiful wedding," Rylee said. "The vows made me cry!"

Gracie didn't say anything, and Adam felt her stiffen beside him. He wanted to reach out and put his arm around her, but he didn't want to do anything that would make her uncomfortable.

In no time, they were pulling into Katie and Sawyer's driveway. The decorated car, which had carried Greg and Sasha, was already parked in the circular driveway and they pulled in behind it. A couple of high school boys directed cars to park in the grassy field that had been designated as the parking lot for the guests.

Adam opened the door and breathed in the fresh air. If he could just get to one of Sawyer's scotch bottles. Sawyer kept a fully stocked bar. He'd never been much of a drinker and Adam knew he wouldn't miss a bottle from his cabinet. Everyone would be outside enjoying themselves on the nice afternoon. No one would notice if he slipped inside. He would go as soon as Greg and Sasha made their entrance, and all eyes were on them.

"Adam?" Bryan said. "Want to help me with the music? I could use a little bit of tuning. My ears are a little tone deaf sometimes."

Adam grimaced. The last thing he wanted to do was help with the music, but he couldn't draw attention to himself either. He needed to act like he always did, helpful and optimistic. He was good at performing a role for his drinking. Adam followed behind Bryan to the back of the barn where they'd set up a system to pipe music throughout the barn and into the main room.

"Can you check that cord over there?" Bryan asked. "I want to make sure everything is connected before we hit play."

Adam leaned down and made sure the long extension cord was plugged into the back of the speaker. He turned and gave Bryan a thumbs-up.

Bryan smiled at him and pressed the small green button. Light piano music came through the speakers and drifted onto the lawn where groups of people clustered, sipping wine, beer, and enjoying appetizers. Adam wished he could be one of those people, easily able to take just one drink in a celebratory fashion at an event. And maybe he could. He'd been sober for five years. He hadn't gone into the liquor store the other day and bought a bottle of alcohol. He'd been able to restrain himself. Maybe things had shifted inside him enough that now he could drink socially. He had heard that your body reset itself every seven years. Maybe now he was a different person. Maybe he could drink now.

"Be right back," Adam said, turning and headed away from the barn.

But he hadn't gone three feet when Seth stopped him. "Adam!"

Seth wore a black suit with a light blue tie. The tie matched Suzanne's dress which was a light blue with a scooped neckline. She wore pearl earrings and a small pearl necklace. Her hand rested in Seth's.

"How was the wedding?"

"Everything went off fine," Adam said. He tried to appear relaxed and calm. "I'm just headed into the house for a minute. Need to get something."

Seth eyed him. "Let's go over there to talk." He placed his hand on Adam's lower back and guided him to a couple hay bales that had been set up as bench seats.

Adam gritted his teeth. The craving washed over him. He had to get to that scotch. He could taste it on his tongue, sliding down his throat. It would take away all his emotions.

"I know you want to drink." Seth lowered his voice. "And I'll tell you that I'm not going to stop you. Whether you drink is up to you. But," Seth said. "I am going to tell you that when you put that drink in your mouth, it won't just be one like you are thinking."

Adam eyed Seth. "You don't think I could just have one drink?"

"No," Seth said. "I don't. It doesn't work like that for us. Alcohol is an addiction, and it will hit your body with a force that you will not be able to control."

Adam knew Seth had relapsed. He said it'd happened for him at five years, just where Adam was now. He'd relapsed and gone back to a 90-day treatment, and he'd stayed sober. But Seth's experience didn't have to be his. He'd heard guys talk about having a couple drinks and not needing to go to treatment. He could do it.

"I appreciate your concern," Adam said. "I'm headed into the house now."

He turned from Seth and strode toward the large sprawling home and the liquor cabinet. Just. One. Drink.

Chapter 20

Gracie leaned down to touch the blister forming on her left heel. She knew she should have worn her pumps around the inn for a few days before wearing them for the wedding.

The newly forming blister stung under her fingers and small droplets of blood appeared.

"That looks like it hurts." Katie walked past her with a tray of small appetizers. "There are some Band Aids in the front bathroom."

"Thanks," Gracie slipped the strap below the blister and limped toward the two-story home. She went through the side door and headed toward the small bathroom off the kitchen. The sound of footsteps made her stop.

"Sawyer?"

No one answered and Gracie frowned. Katie kept the home open for family to come and go during the party. Robberies and other crimes didn't happen often in Cranberry Bay. But something inside Gracie dropped in her stomach. *Stop*, she shook herself. She was just being silly. She'd read too many mystery books lately.

Inside the small bathroom, Gracie opened a drawer on the left-hand side of a small cabinet. A stack of Band-Aids was arranged neatly inside a small pink basket. She pulled one out and sat down on the toilet. In minutes, she had her shoe off and the Band-Aid placed over the blister.

The clink of ice in a glass startled her. Who was in the house? Katie and Sawyer had made it clear the reception was in the barn and the large sweeping yard.

She stepped out of the bathroom and rounded the corner. Adam stood at the bar. A glass full of ice in front of him and a bottle of Scotch in his left hand.

"Gracie." His eyes widened.

"Adam," Gracie said, her heart pounding. "What are you…"

"I'm having a drink," Adam said. "It's okay." He smiled at her. "It's just one. I can have one sometimes."

Something inside Gracie snapped. A feeling she hadn't had since she was with her ex-fiancé. She knew Adam was lying to her, to himself. Alcoholism was a disease. An alcoholic couldn't just have one drink. It was a compulsion. She'd learned that in her therapy sessions. She remembered her ex-fiancé. Memories she had pushed out of her mind. The way he always kept bottles of liquor tucked into places around the house. How, when she would find them, she would tell him he had a problem with drinking. The way when he hit her, he had always been drinking.

Adam poured the alcohol over the ice.

Gracie turned. She couldn't watch Adam drink. She couldn't see who he would become when he drank. She had to leave now. She had to leave and never look back. Never want to have something more with Adam. There would be nothing more with Adam.

Chapter 21

Adam couldn't stop staring at the spot where Gracie had just been. The way her face looked, her eyes vacant. Worst of all was seeing the trust she'd placed in him crumbling to the floor like bricks in an earthquake. He pushed the drink away from him.

"Adam!" Sawyer stepped into the room. "What are you doing? You got into my liquor cabinet. I should have locked it up!"

"No," Adam said, his voice defeated. "It wouldn't have mattered. If I couldn't get the drink here, I would have gotten it somewhere else."

Adam sank to the floor, putting his head between his hands. "I didn't know it would be this hard."

Sawyer sank down on the floor beside him. "What can I do?"

"You can't do anything," Adam said. "It's me. It's this urge to drink when things get too much."

"Is it leaving Cranberry Bay?" Sawyer asked. "Is that why you were going to drink?"

"Yes." Adam dropped his voice. "I asked Gracie to go with me, but she didn't answer me. I was wrong to hope she would go with me." And now he knew she would never answer. She had seen him with a drink in his hand. She didn't know he hadn't taken a sip. He knew her story. He knew her history with her ex. He had taken the one thing she had given to him, her trust, and betrayed her. He had proven that he couldn't be the man she needed, just like with the kayak accident.

"Love is tricky," Sawyer said. "It's not a straight road. It's up and down and you have to do a lot of compromise."

"I can't even get out the gate," Adam said. "I've never felt like I do about Gracie with anyone else. And I'm scared."

"I was, too," Sawyer said. "I still am. Love isn't anything like business. In business, I know how things work. I set goals. I do the work to achieve those goals. But love…" He shook his head. "There's nothing like that."

"How do you do it?" Adam asked. "How do you stay with your heart and not get scared and run away?"

Sawyer rubbed his hands on his slacks. He looked away, toward the piano where pictures decorated every space. "What other choice is there?" he asked. "After Ginger died, I swore I was never going to fall in love again. Not if it came to the amount of pain I felt, the pain of losing someone. And I kept my resolve. But then

Katie came along, and I just couldn't imagine life without her in it."

Sawyer patted his shoulder. "Sometimes you just have to leap because you can't imagine life any other way."

Adam nodded. He hadn't taken the leap. He'd taken a small jump over a puddle when he asked Gracie to move with him. But that wasn't taking the big leap. The big leap was asking Gracie to marry him. Asking her to break the vow they had made to each other that marriage wasn't for either one of them. Something inside of him shifted and settled. He wanted to spend the rest of his life with Gracie. He didn't just want her to move with him.

But he knew his disease of alcoholism could only be controlled one day at a time. The craving would always be there, bubbling under the surface, threatening to take out everything he had. Sobriety always had to come first or he had nothing.

"Sawyer?" Katie's voice called through the house. "Where are the extra plates? I thought we had them in the barn, but I can't find them."

Sawyer stood. He placed his hands on the counter and looked down at Adam. "I can't stop you from taking that drink," he said. "But I can tell you this as your brother. I want you to be happy. I want you to be happy with the woman you love and if you take that drink, you will lose her. And," Sawyer paused. His voice hardened. "None of us will ever allow Maddie to go with you if you are drinking."

Adam nodded. He knew that Sawyer spoke the truth. His family would protect Maddie if he drank again. He would not want Maddie to move to Montana and watch him descend into his alcoholism.

"Uncle Adam?" Maddie's voice rose from the porch. "We need another person to play croquet!"

Adam stood. If he drank, he would let down the family who loved him and who he loved. And he was going to try with everything he had not to do that. Seth was right. He needed to make sure he was going to AA meetings regularly, keeping his mind clear with meditation and prayer.

But he could do it. He knew he could. He could be the man his family wanted him to be. And, he straightened his shoulders, he could be the man Gracie needed. He walked to the sink and poured the liquid out of the glass.

"I'm on my way!" Adam strode to the open patio door. "I call the red balls!"

Chapter 22

Gracie pushed her way through the guests. She walked past Maddie, who was setting up a game of croquet.

"Gracie!" Maddie said. "Do you want to play?"

"I don't think so," Gracie said. "I'm going to head back to the inn. I just got a call that there's a guest who is trying to check in a little early." The lie slipped out easily. She couldn't stay at the wedding reception. She didn't want to see Adam after he'd been drinking. She *couldn't* see him after he'd been drinking. She wanted to always remember him as he was—sober and kind.

Gracie hurried to the side room of the barn. But before she could get there, she bumped into Rylee.

"Gracie?" Rylee peered at her. "Is everything okay?"

"No," Gracie said, shaking her head and holding back tears.

"Come on." Rylee grabbed her arm and pulled her

over to the side of the barn, away from the musicians and dance floor. She guided her to a small bench.

"Is something wrong at the inn?"

"No." Gracie shook her head. A small tear dropped out of her eye and down her cheek. "It's Adam. I went into the house to get a Band-Aid for my blister, and he was pouring a drink."

Rylee's face paled. "I'm sorry, Gracie."

"It's okay," Gracie said, shaking her head. The tears dropped down her face. "It's not really. He asked me to move with him to Montana and I realized I didn't just want to move with him. I wanted a commitment. A marriage commitment."

"But…" Rylee squeezed her hand.

"But I can't tell him that now. Not after I saw him drinking. I don't want to see who he becomes when he's drunk."

Rylee exhaled. "You know my dad was a gambling addict."

Gracie studied Rylee. She had never talked to Rylee about her story with her ex-fiancé. She didn't know much about Rylee's dad. She only knew that Rylee came to Cranberry Bay when she'd inherited her grandmother's house and had reconnected with her high school sweetheart, Bryan.

"He gambled my whole life," Rylee said. "It's hard to love an addict."

"My ex- fiancé was an addict," Gracie said. "And he hit me." She knew Rylee would understand the ups and downs, the hoping someone would change.

"I'm sorry," Rylee said and hugged Gracie. "I knew there was something more about your past, but I never wanted to press you until you were ready to talk about it."

"I thought Adam was different. I thought he wasn't like my ex- fiancé." Gracie's chest felt heavy. She had believed Adam was different than Mike. He was gentle and kind to her and everyone in Cranberry Bay. She'd never seen him get mad and raise his voice or hit anyone.

"I understand," Rylee said. "Love is always a risk."

Tears poured down Gracie's face. She loved Adam and she didn't want to lose him. But she couldn't watch him drink. She couldn't be part of his life if he was drinking and trust that the abuse that happened with her ex-fiancé wouldn't happen again.

"I know sometimes we think the same thing will happen," Rylee said. "We think that if we open ourselves up to loving someone that we will be disappointed, that the pain will come. I know I thought that with Bryan. But you have to give people a chance to prove you wrong, too."

Gracie nodded. She understood what Rylee was saying. She hadn't seen Adam drink the alcohol. She didn't know what had happened after she left the kitchen.

"What are you two talking about so seriously?" Rebecca Shuster carried a pink lemonade in her hand and strode up beside them. Her long pink dress flowed around her legs, and she wore a soft cream-colored shawl.

"I saw Adam pouring a drink," Gracie said. She knew her words would upset Adam's mom, but she had to tell the truth.

Rebecca's face paled. She took a deep breath and sat down beside Gracie. "I love my son more than anything in the world," Rebecca said and smoothed her hands over her dress. "But his alcoholism is his disease. None of us can control whether he drinks or not."

"You sound so wise," Gracie said, wiping a tear away from her cheek.

"Adam's counselors recommended I go to Al-Anon. It's support for friends and family members of alcoholics, whether the alcoholic is still drinking or not," Rebecca said. "I wanted to do everything I could to help my son."

"And did you help him?" Gracie asked.

"What I learned," Rebecca said, "is that I can't control Adam's disease of alcoholism. I can't cure it, and I can't change it." She took a sip of her lemonade.

"That sounds logical," Gracie said, nodding.

"It's very logical," Rebecca said. "But it can be very hard to do without support. I attend a weekly Al-Anon meeting in Sea Shore Cove if you'd like to go with me."

Gracie nodded. "I think that might be helpful. Adam's not the first person I've loved with a drinking problem. I would like to know more about it."

"We'll go," Rebecca said. She patted Gracie's arm. "We both love him."

The sound of laughter and the crack of the croquet balls filled the air.

Gracie turned to see a red ball moving quickly across the ground and into the small metal hoop.

"Point for Adam!" Maddie said, her voice high and clear.

Adam waved his stick in the air and turned to look at her.

Chapter 23

"Point for you." Sawyer patted him on the back.

Adam turned away from Gracie. "Sawyer," he said. "I need a favor."

"Of course," Sawyer said. "What do you need?"

"I've got temporary housing lined up that is a part of my job. But," Adam paused. "I want to find a property that's bigger."

"What do you have in mind?" Sawyer studied him.

"Something that could be turned into a bed and breakfast or small inn."

"I see." The grin broke across Sawyer's face. "This wouldn't have anything to do with a certain someone?" Sawyer nodded toward Gracie.

"Maybe," Adam said, and hope bubbled inside him. He wanted to prove to her he could be the man she needed. He would provide and protect her. He would honor her goals and support her in whatever made her happy.

"Let me see what I can do." Sawyer nodded his head. "I've got a few connections in Montana. I'm guessing you'll want a separate space for Maddie, too?"

"Yes," Adam said. "Nothing like what you've got here." He waved his hand toward the expansive property. "But something Gracie could love, just like the New Leaf Inn." He cleared his throat. It wasn't just Gracie who loved the New Leaf Inn. He loved it, too. He loved helping her prepare the backyard for the wedding, the way they worked together so effortlessly. He wanted to work with her on another project they both loved.

"Did someone lose a red croquet ball?" Gracie's voice called out over the yard, high and clear.

"That's mine." Adam strode toward her. He stopped in front of Gracie as she bent over and picked up the ball. She held it out, and his fingers touched hers as he lifted it from her.

"Gracie," Adam said. "I know you saw me with a drink. But I poured that drink out. I didn't take a sip."

Gracie studied him. Her eyes searched his face.

"You don't have to believe me," Adam said. "But I hope you will." He hoped with all his heart that Gracie would believe him. He loved her, and he wanted her to trust him, but he knew trust didn't come easily. Especially when that trust had been broken by past betrayals.

"Uncle Adam!" Maddie called. "We're ready for your turn."

"Coming!" Adam gave Gracie another look, turned and strode back to the game. Building trust began with being honest.

Seth grinned at him. "You're behind now. I just scored a point."

Adam grimaced and took his place behind the red ball. The game finished in minutes with him scoring third behind Maddie and Seth.

Seth patted him on the back. "I'm proud of you. It's not easy to walk away from the urge to drink."

Adam nodded. "I let my feelings get the best of me."

"Feelings are scary," Seth said. "Big feelings like love."

Adam felt his ears redden.

"It's all out of our control," Seth said. "The feeling of falling in love, wondering if they love you back. And if they do, that's even more scary than if they don't."

"I never realized how scary it could be," Adam said.

"Because love has never hit you when you are sober," Seth said.

"Gracie saw me with the drink."

"Be honest with her about everything. Especially your feelings. It's the only way through all of this." Seth patted him on the back. "You can do this."

A burst of laughter came from across the yard. Gracie stood with Katie, Rylee, and Sasha, all of them laughing.

In that minute, she turned and looked directly at him, her eyes shining and bright, and she smiled.

"Go on," Seth said and pushed toward Gracie.

Adam nodded and walked across the grass. He felt like a high school kid, unsure and walking to the girl he loved more than anything to ask her for a dance.

"Gracie?" Adam touched her arm. "Want to take a walk?"

Gracie turned to him, her eyes bright. "Yes."

Adam guided Gracie toward the edge of the lawn where a small trail led down to a vintage RV. Katie was working on rehabbing the inside for a client. Gracie walked beside him. They'd walked together so often their rhythm fell into place naturally. Adam took a deep breath. He could talk to Gracie about anything. She didn't judge him. She never judged him. It was one of the things he loved best about her.

"Every day I get up and pray for another day sober. But I've been feeling overwhelmed." He exhaled. "All these changes, getting the new job and," he paused, "my feelings for you."

Gracie stopped. She turned to look at him. "I have feelings for you, too."

Adam stepped closer to her. "I want you to come with me to Montana."

Gracie's face tightened.

"No," Adam said. "I'm not saying this right."

"I can't go to Montana with you…"

Adam's chest constricted. He felt the bottom drop out from underneath him. His heart pounded. "Gracie, I…"

"We said neither of us wanted to get married. But something changed and I did want to get married. But then," Gracie stopped. "I saw how close to drinking you came. And it scared me."

"I understand," Adam said. He knew it was asking a

lot for Gracie to trust him, and he knew he couldn't force that, as much as he wanted her.

Gracie leaned over. She placed a small kiss on his cheek. "I love you, Adam. But I need to trust myself that I will make the right choice this time." She gathered her dress in her hand, turned and walked away.

Chapter 24

On Monday, Gracie hurried down the beach to the group of people clustered at the water's edge. A cat carrier sat on the sand ahead of her. She left Max at home, knowing it wouldn't be good to have a dog at a bird release.

She'd attended the noon Al-Anon meeting with Rebecca Shuster and found herself warmly included in a group of people who understood alcoholism. They'd read from one of the books, and the words of love, understanding, and compassion washed over Gracie. Love and compassion for both the alcoholic and the ones who loved them. There was no fear or judgement, just a kind understanding as people went around the circle and shared their experiences, strength and hope.

Gracie approached the small group. Lisa stepped over and threw her arm around the shoulder. "I'm so glad you could come!"

Gracie smiled. She wouldn't have missed the puffin

release. Adam knelt beside the carrier. He looked up at her. "Do you want to open the cage?"

Gracie nodded and stepped forward. She knelt beside Adam. Their fingers touched as she lifted the top of the crate.

The puffin fluffed its wings. Adam reached in and grabbed it around the middle. He lifted it out of the crate and held it out from his body.

"Let her go!" Lisa said and lifted her hands to the sky.

Adam walked to the edge of the water and set the puffin down on the sand. They never just tossed a bird into the air and expected it to fly. It took a minute for the bird to adjust itself to being back outside and that it wasn't confined anymore.

The puffin shook itself and then flapped its wings a couple times. In minutes, it was lifting off into the sky, the wings fluttering as it headed toward the large sea stack and the nesting burrows atop.

"That's it," Lisa said and wiped a small tear out of the corner of her eye. "It gets me every time to see them released."

Gracie knew the feeling and wiped a tear away from her own eye. She turned to find Adam's outstretched hand, offering a tissue.

Gracie took the tissue and wiped her eyes. She swallowed what felt like a wall of tears. "When I first came to Cranberry Bay, I was like the puffin. I was injured and afraid. But in Cranberry Bay, I found myself again. I learned to love and be loved."

"Cranberry Bay is a special place," Adam said. "I'm going to miss it."

She touched his arm. "You are one of the people who I love. But now it's time to fly again. It's time to be like that puffin. It's time to trust myself and our love."

Adam stepped toward her. His eyes bright and shining. "I have something to show you." He pulled out his phone from his back pocket. "It's a new listing that Sawyer sent me this morning."

Gracie gasped. It wasn't just a listing for a home for Adam. It was a bed and breakfast.

"The two-story log home has been a bed and breakfast for twenty years. The couple is retiring. There's also a small one-room cottage on the property." Adam scrolled through the picture on his phone.

"There are owner's quarters on the second floor. They are bigger than what I have now." Gracie studied the details on each picture.

"Yes," Adam said. "But you don't have to live in them. The property is adjacent to a home that is also for sale. Our home."

"Our home?" Gracie said and swallowed.

"Our home." Adam reached into his pocket and held out a simple gold ring. "Gracie, will you marry me?"

Joy surged in Gracie. The joy of watching the puffin release into the wild. The joy of having the man she loved in front of her. The man she would take the risk with and trust, the man she would love in sickness and in health, and trust not just in Adam, but most of all she trusted herself.

And she wasn't alone. She had the love of her Cranberry Bay friends and Adam's family would now be her family, and together they would all have the strength to love. Sometimes love needed a team to support it, and she had one. A good one. "Yes," Gracie said. She reached down and hugged him. "I will."

Adam stood and gathered Gracie into his arms. He pulled her close and she stepped into his tender embrace, feeling the love pouring from him to her.

Epilogue

A light early September rain fell on the front windows of the New Leaf Inn. Gracie handed the keys of the inn to Aunt Celia. Her heart was heavy but at the same time a hopefulness and lightness filled her.

For the last few weeks, she'd worked hard training Aunt Celia on all the procedures but had quickly realized she was a natural. The guests loved Aunt Celia and the one or two who caused problems, Aunt Celia firmly put them in their place and established she was running the inn and what she said was the law of the land.

It didn't take long for Aunt Celia to put her St. Louis house on the market and got a full price offer. She signed the sale papers and bought New Leaf Inn, and with the proceeds that were left after she paid off the bad investment.

"This time I know I'm investing in a good thing," she'd said to Gracie.

"Ready?" Adam touched her shoulder. He'd returned to Cranberry Bay for a few days to help her pack up her things and together, they would drive back to Montana. Maddie would join them in another few weeks after her work at the Wildlife Center was over for the season.

"Yes," Gracie said. Her silver engagement ring sparkled in the sunlight. Adam had given her his mother's engagement ring, a simple gold band which would be joined with another solid one when they married at Christmas. A wedding filled with snow in Montana where everyone from Cranberry Bay would come over to enjoy the festivities. Adam had already lined up a horse and carriage ride and all her friends promised to help her with the best wedding ever.

And best of all, everyone could stay at their new bed and breakfast, Mountain View Inn.

In the last few days, Gracie had said her good-byes. First to the women in the sewing circle, knowing that she was becoming a sister-in-law to Katie and Rylee and that although it was goodbye to their weekly sewing circles, it wasn't goodbye forever. She'd be a member of the Shuster family.

She'd walked the beach trails one final time with Max, knowing he would love the spacious yard in Montana and new hiking trails but at the same time as the cool winds brushed over her cheeks, she felt the sadness of leaving the wide expansive ocean behind that she'd come to love and which had healed her. But that was what change was about—it was leaving the old and starting off on a new journey.

"I'm ready." She turned and smiled at Adam. A new adventure awaited with the man she loved.

New Leaf Inn Peanut Butter Chocolate Chip Oatmeal Cookies

2 Eggs

    1 C Peanut Butter

    1/3 C Pure Maple Syrup

    1 ½ C rolled oats

    ½ tsp baking soda

    ½ tsp ground cinnamon

    ½ tsp sea salt

    1 tsp vanilla (optional)

    ½ cups walnuts

Preheat the oven to 350. Line a baking sheet with parchment paper. Whisk the eggs in a mixing bowl until they are well-beaten, Add in the peanut butter and pure maple syrup to the large bowl and stir until the wet ingredients are well-combined. Stir in the dry ingredients (oats, cinnamon, baking soda and sea salt) until a thick, sticky dough forms.

Mix in the chocolate chips. Drop in ball shapes onto

the baking sheet. Bake for 9 to 12 minutes or until the cookies appear stet up. About ten minutes. Allow the cookies to cool for ten minutes before serving. Store in airtight container in the refrigerator for five days or freeze in a large zip lock freezer bag for up to three months.

Wedding Punch

Wedding Punch

1 ½ C orange juice
   2 C cranberry juice cocktail
   1 C pomegranate juice
   1 ½ C Ginger Ale

Mix all ingredients in a pitcher. Place in the refrigerator and serve cold.

Acknowledgements

Dear Reader,

A big thank you to my team who continues to make sure my books are the best stories they can be. Su Kopil at Earthly Charms for creating the best covers ever, Bev Katz Rosenbaum who always encourages me to dig just a little deeper into the story with her developmental edits, and Casey Harris-Parks at Heart Full of Ink who cleans up the errors in her copy edits. And to the Rose City Romance Writers Monday Night Group, I could not do it without you!

The Wildlife Center of the North Coast was a huge inspiration for this story. If you'd like to learn more about the seabirds rescued visit their website: https://coast wildlife.org/

If someone you love has a drinking problem, you can find out more about Al-Anon here: https://al-anon.org/. Or if you are struggling with a drinking problem you can find out more about AA here: https://www.aa.org/.

Acknowledgements

This book concludes the Cranberry Bay Romance series. I started this series in 2015 with *Sweetheart Cottage* and created the small town from my passion and love of the North Oregon Coast. In 2023 and 2024, the series surprised me with two holiday romances, *Sweetheart Christmas* and *Sweetheart Santa*, as it was only intended to be a three-book series. When I started writing *Sweetheart Wedding*, I knew this book would end the series, and Gracie would have to make a choice about whether to leave or stay in Cranberry Bay. I wasn't sure what she would choose but as the story unfolded, I knew both Adam and Gracie would choose love.

If you have read one or the entire Cranberry Bay series, thank you!

All my best,
Mindy Hardwick

About the Author

Mindy Hardwick holds an MFA in Writing for Children and Young Adults from Vermont College. Her published contemporary small-town heartwarming romance includes her Cranberry Bay Series: *Sweetheart Cottage, Sweetheart Summer, Sweetheart Christmas* and *Sweetheart Santa*. She has also published a young adult romance, *Weaving Magic* and a young adult novella, *Erin's Choice*.

Mindy's middle grade books include: *The World is a Sniff, Stained Glass Summer, Some Stories Are Not Seen, and Seymour's Secret*. Mindy facilitated a poetry workshop for teens at Denney Juvenile Justice Center and wrote about the experience in her memoir, *Kids in Orange: Voices from Juvenile Detention*.

Mindy can often be found walking on the north Oregon Coast beaches. Visit her website: www. mindy-hardwick.com to find out about new releases, upcoming events or to book her to speak to your class or school group.

Sign up for her newsletter here

Also by Mindy Hardwick

<u>Middle Grade</u>

Stained Glass Summer

Some Stories Are Not Seen

The World Is a Sniff

Seymour's Secret

<u>Young Adult</u>

Weaving Magic

Kids In Orange: Voices from Juvenile Detention

Erin's Choice

<u>Sweet Contemporary Romance</u>

Sweetheart Cottage

Sweetheart Summer

Sweetheart Christmas

Sweetheart Santa

Sweetheart Wedding

Sweetheart Santa

Chapter 1

Greg maneuvered his Rivian R1S into a parking spot at the dark marina. He'd made it to Cranberry Bay in record time, thanks to the Rivian's blistering ability to hit sixty mph in three seconds and a smooth ride without traffic from Seattle. The five-hour trip could easily turn into seven or eight with gridlock on I-5.

A couple fishing boats bobbed in the water, each tied to a buoy instead of a C-hook. Dock boards angled toward the water and a few floated along the shoreline. A seagull perched on the top of a piling with splintered wood. Near the road a small building tilted to the side, the windows and door missing.

Sawyer had warned him the marina would be a big project, but he'd get a good price. Price was no object to Greg. The fortune he'd amassed in Bitcoin and reinvested in other markets continued to make him one of the wealthiest men in Seattle, outside the tech giants like Bill Gates and Paul Allen. But something inside him wanted something else, something more. Something he couldn't name. A restlessness had taken hold of him, keeping him up at night as he lay in his multi-million-dollar home staring at the blinking lights of downtown Seattle.

He loved investing in Bitcoin in the early days, the excitement of waking up every morning not quite knowing how the markets would roll, the challenge, the risk. But that was gone now. He sold all his shares and reinvested it into real estate portfolios with his financial team who kept him informed of every move but rarely allowed him to get his hands into the mix. The marina purchase would allow him a chance to actually be involved with one of his investments.

Greg stepped out of the car and a blast of cold wind hit his face. He ducked back inside and grabbed his Burberry Puffer jacket from the backseat. He was used to the rainy Pacific Northwest winters living in Seattle, but the cold, wet damp on the Oregon Coast was a different beast. It seeped into his skin, making him long to cuddle up in front of a cozy fire with someone he loved.

But there wasn't anyone. His marriage to Jennifer dragged itself through frosty silent nights until finally they parted. He'd casually dated after his divorce, but nothing filled the empty inside, and he'd become disillusioned trying to fend off women who wanted his money rather than him. He cared about Jennifer, but he had never been in love with her. That once in a lifetime love had been tucked away in a place he never revisited. A time with a girl who'd had his heart. A girl who had left and he'd never followed her, not because he didn't want to but because he believed he represented everything she'd lost.

He tried to be a good husband to Jennifer and bought a large sweeping multi-story home overlooking Lake Washington, a high-powered motorboat, and expensive vacations in Hawaii. But it hadn't been enough. She'd divorced him and found someone new before the divorce papers were finalized. The last he'd heard, they were expecting their first child.

Now, he was here, standing in the parking lot of a run-down marina, in a small town on the Oregon Coast just days after Thanksgiving. It wasn't even one of the more expensive beach towns, but a small, one-stop-sign town that most people drove through on their way to somewhere else. The sleeting rain slapped against the car as he tried to find a new purpose, something meaningful in his life.

"Greg!"

Sawyer stepped out of a low one-story flat roof building. A strand of red and green blinking Christmas lights framed the doorway, and a ladder perched to the side while a long strand of garland and a wreath leaned against the building. A small sign hung above the door that read, Bill's Tavern. Sawyer wore jeans and a red fleece sweatshirt and waved at Greg.

Greg hustled toward the open door and the light and warmth pooled onto the front porch. He'd met Sawyer at an investing conference. The hit it off and when Sawyer traveled to Seattle for business, the two enjoyed playing golf and trading investing tips.

"We're really having a winter storm," Sawyer said. A gust of wind grabbed hold of the door. Sawyer held on to the handle while Greg hustled past him and inside.

Greg shook the rain off his jacket and unzipped it. A chalkboard advertised different types of craft beer and a couple of people sat at the bar. White Christmas lights framed the large mirror above the bar and strands of green garland draped along the edges of the counter.

Women's laughter drifted to him and filled the room with joy. He turned to a small table where four women were sharing a large plate of nachos. The women ranged in age from eighteen to sixtyish. All of them had a fresh, wholesome, girl next door look that he didn't see in his social circles very often. The women he knew were always polished with heavy make-up, hair that received hours of straightening, and clothing that cost a fortune. The group at the table looked as if they could have walked out of a day of teaching at a middle or elementary school. Each wore a colorful scarf wrapped over a simple top and jeans. Their hair was short or tied back with clips and their eyes sparkled.

"That's Katie, my wife." Sawyer nodded toward the table. The pride evident in his voice. "My younger sister, Lisa, her daughter Maddie, and my mom, Rebecca."

As if on cue, Katie rose and walked to Sawyer. She looped her right arm through his and smiled. Love pooled in her eyes.

Greg swallowed. Only one woman had ever looked at him the way Katie looked at Sawyer. One woman he had never forgotten. A woman he'd never tried to find, not because he didn't want to but because her leaving had been so sudden, so painful, that he couldn't bear adding more pain to her life or his.

"Katie, this is Greg. He wants to buy the marina and invest in Cranberry Bay."

Katie held out her hand. "Cranberry Bay is a good investment. It may not look like much, but we're slowly getting things turned around here."

"Katie owns a very successful fabric shop. She ships all over the country and people come from Seattle and Portland for quilt fabric and her weekend retreats."

A pretty blush spread across Katie's cheeks. "Sawyer and I were competitors. His big box store on the edge of town pushed my downtown fabric store out of business. But," she smiled at him, "we worked through our differences. I have a wonderful space on the edge of town. The Red Barn? You may have seen it?"

"I don't think so." Greg shook his head. He didn't have the heart to admit he hadn't paid attention to much except his playlist on his drive into Cranberry Bay.

"I've got the numbers on the marina for you." Sawyer lowered his voice. "I think you saw what you'll be getting into. My brother, Bryan, is our town's real estate agent. He ran some comps for you. You just need to name your price."

"I'd like to see those numbers." Greg wanted to pay fair value.

"Of course," Sawyer said. "Wouldn't expect less of you."

Greg's stomach rumbled and he inhaled the scent of hamburgers. "How are the burgers?"

"Grass fed, organic," Katie said. "You can't go wrong." She touched Sawyer's arm with her left hand. Her fingers caressed his lower forearm. "Your Mom needs a little help getting her holiday decorations down from the attic."

"I'll stop by after I finish up here," Sawyer said. "Thanks for letting me know."

Katie stood on her tiptoes and Sawyer leaned down and kissed her.

Greg's stomach contracted. He'd left his family as soon as he started college, getting a small apartment, and working a part-time job designing websites to cover his rent. After he invested in Bitcoin and money poured in, he sent checks to his mom but always found excuses for why he couldn't return to upstate New York for the holidays. Painful family memories haunted him.

At Christmas, Jennifer tried to make their home something out of a magazine and they had a roster of fund investors attend the parties. He usually wrote a large check to a couple non-profits and requested his name be kept anonymous. It seemed easier that way. Easier to forget the times he'd spent as a child going to food banks with his mom.

"*We will never talk about this,*" she'd instructed him. And it wasn't just the food bank. It was the late night talks he heard between his parents, their voices strained, tense, and loud as they argued over which bill to pay. The house too leveraged with primary and secondary loans, the leased car payments, the credit card bills. No one talked about why his dad lost his job or the visits from the police and lawyers.

When the ruling was made he went to jail for embezzlement, the family lied and said he was on an extended business trip overseas. They were secrets Greg tucked deep inside, the scars he showed no one except Sasha.

The first girl he loved.

During the late nights, curled together in his bed, and he'd told her everything. She listened while he talked, held him while he cried, and encouraged him when he'd declared he would carve his path, a path of success and not failure. And he'd done that. He'd become wealthy, but success hadn't been enough to fill the empty place inside him. The place inside him that craved someone to love.

Christmas morning always dawned hollow and empty. It never held what he really craved—love and someone who felt like home. There had only been one person who made him feel that way. One person he tried not to think about but who crept along the edges of his memories, haunting him with what might have been if he had followed her and believed more in the heart and not so much in crushing that aching emptiness from his childhood of trying to overcome his dad's failures.

Sawyer stepped up to the bar and placed an order for two burgers and a couple beers.

"There's a table over there." He motioned toward a small round table in the corner of the room.

Greg took his beer and followed Sawyer. Sawyer

moved through the room, nodding and smiling to everyone.

When they reached the table, Greg pulled out a chair and sat down. "Good to see you again." He'd met Sawyer a few years ago in Seattle at a large-scale investor conference. The two had struck up a conversation and hit it off. Sawyer sent him listings of potential business opportunities ever since. Nothing caught his eye until the marina came on the market. He'd been sailing since he was a teen in the waters of Lake Ontario in upstate New York. Sailing was his place of refuge. He loved sailing to the San Juan Islands every summer and spending the long summer nights eating fresh fish he'd caught. Jennifer never liked to sail, and after the divorce, Greg sold the large motorboat she wanted and returned to his love of sailing.

Sawyer chuckled. "Cheers. It'll be great to have you in Cranberry Bay."

Greg raised his glass. "First let's get the marina bought." Greg had no intention of staying in Cranberry Bay. He just wanted to invest in something he could see progressing. Something outside his investments managed so carefully by his finance team. But he wasn't fooling himself. He wouldn't live in a town like Cranberry Bay. Small towns meant everyone knew your business. He liked his privacy. A lot. He'd hire someone to run the marina and a contractor to bring it back to working order. He'd make a point to visit Cranberry Bay once a year, most likely in the summer and check on things, maybe stay in the nearby upscale beach town in a suite overlooking the Pacific Ocean. But he'd never live in Cranberry Bay.

In Seattle, he relished his privacy and could easily find a restaurant or bar where he'd be anonymous. Tech guys were a dime a dozen and he slid in and out of the smaller bars and restaurants on the east side of Seattle, skipping the flashy expensive Lake Washington restaurants in Kirkland where he'd once gone with Jennifer and people recognized him.

Sawyer reached into his satchel and pulled out a manilla envelope. He slipped out a single sheet of paper and slid it across the table. "Here you go. The comps."

"Not much to compare, eh?" Greg said, his eyes slid over the single sheet.

"Sorry," Sawyer said. "We don't have many marinas around here that go on the market. The ocean waters are too rough and unprotected for small craft boats and sailboats. Most of the smaller boats go out of the marinas further down the highway where the bay comes in and is a little more protected."

Greg tucked the paper into his pocket. "I'll write up a couple bid options for you."

Sawyer took a sip of his beer. "Where are you staying? We'd love to have you at our place for dinner."

"I got a room at the Inn," Greg said. "It seems like it's the only place?"

"The River Rock Inn is great too. It's a set of old fishing cottages that my brother's wife restored. My brother, Bryan, runs them with his wife, Rylee. "

"I'll remember that for next time." Greg took a sip of his beer. Light just the way he liked his craft ale.

A tall, thin woman slid two thick burgers in front of them. She wiped her hands on a red apron tied around her waist over jeans and a green, long-sleeved top. She wore a red Santa hat and small bell earrings dangled from her ears. "Be sure to stop in the Lazy Dayz bakery. If you go in the morning, you'll find most of the local crew enjoying coffee and pastries." She smiled at him and winked. "Can I get you anything else?"

"Will do," Greg said. He didn't want to encourage the glint in her eyes and, he sensed, the hope of something more. He preferred to keep to himself and not engage with too many people unless there was a specific purpose. He'd always let Jennifer do their socializing. He didn't have a profile on the multitudes of social media channels that were so popular.

He picked up the burger and took a bite. Thick juice dripped down his chin. "This is a pretty good burger," he said through mouthfuls.

"This place is on the Coast Highway Food Trail. I think you'll find that about Cranberry Bay," Sawyer said. "We may not look like much but give us a chance and we'll surprise you."

Greg nodded. He wasn't planning to stick around long enough to find out anything about Cranberry Bay. As soon as he wrapped up the purchase of the marine and hired a manager and contractor he'd be gone.

Find out more about Sweetheart Santa and the Cranberry Bay series here.

www.ingramcontent.com/pod-product-compliance
Lightning Source LLC
Chambersburg PA
CBHW060310310726
48976CB00007B/2277